THE OTHER SIDE

Finding the Greener Grass

Paul D Raymond

Point Rider Publishing®

The Other Side: *Finding the Greener Grass*
By Paul Raymond

Cover and Interior Design: Brooke Rousseau, BA Graphic Design
Cover Font "Moon Flower": Denise Bentulan

Point Rider Publishing ®
www.point-rider-publishing.com

ISBN-13: 978-0-692-37519-8
LCCN: 2015931560

Printed in the United States of America

I would like to dedicate this book to my wife Connie, our four children and their spouses; Brent & Vesbein, Blair & Christie, Kristy & Jeff, Lori & Brent, and to those who consider me their friend.

"It is the task of the enlightened not only to ascend to learning and to see the good but to be willing to descend again to those prisoners and to share their troubles and their honors, whether they are worth having or not. And this they must do, even with the prospect of death."

~ The Allegory of the Cave, Plato

TABLE OF CONTENTS

From the publisher...

When author Paul Raymond asked me to write something for his book, it was an easy request to fulfill. I'm a big fan of books that offer insight. Regardless of the topic and genre, I like to see a positive outcome to an internal dilemma. Paul Raymond's *The Other Side* is one such book.

With the state our planet is in, it is easy to find ourselves complacent with less-than-healthy behaviors and ideals. No matter what group in which we may find ourselves, mob mentality can weave its way into the fabric of the community. We learn what we live, and we live what we know. Sometimes, we are forced to step away from the chaos — around us *and* within us — to see just what we think and feel. There are perceptions skewed by internal and external factors, and perceptions create stereotypes.

I dislike immensely when someone claims I am something I am not; positive or negative, I don't like to be labeled and boxed-in to a false perception. This is why *The Other Side* has struck a chord with me.

Paul has written a charming, transparent, and thought-provoking look into one man's perceptions of various people and lifestyles. The ease with which he writes is reminiscent of days past, a refreshing change from the clamor of life in the 21st Century.

More than anything, *The Other Side* helps us peek into our own views without the fear we are the only ones who have pre-conceived ideas about others. The pot of gold in Paul's book is recognizing who experiences the most harm when we cast our perceptions on others.

It is my privilege to introduce you to *The Other Side: Finding the Greener Grass.*

Yvonne Rousseau
Author/Owner/Publisher

PROLOGUE

12

In his formative years, Gary developed interest in observing people, with respect to their attitudes and mannerisms, a practice which would continue for the rest of his life. Early in his youth, he soon discovered that people from the culture in which he was raised (rural America) seemed less sophisticated, less educated and less affluent than those "city dwellers" he saw on the other side of the fence. Conversely, he saw city life as the place to be. The residences there were usually clean and neat.

No, from Gary's point of view, comparing it to city life, there was no value to life on the farm — it was not fun nor carefree. After all, in the city there were no chicken coops to clean, no sprinklers to change, no hay to stack; no beets to thin, no potatoes to pick; no calves to feed; cows to milk; in town there was no livestock that had to be chased in the middle of the night when they broke down the fence, and no manure to walk through. Best of all, no events to miss as a result of those priorities that were seemingly more pressing at home.

On the farm, Gary had to wear old dirty clothes to do chores and that embarrassed him when company came. For the next several years, Gary would see the environment he lived in during his upbringing as a disadvantage or even a handicap to his progression in life. This perception subtly and slowly created a chip on Gary's shoulder. Seeing people in town, who were business owners, doctors, bankers, and lawyers wearing suits and nice clothes, and driving nice cars caused Gary to be jealous and even more resentful of his own surroundings.

As time went by, Gary developed a somewhat unhealthy, sarcastic personality, which, unprovoked and unrehearsed could be unleashed on anyone or anything. Surprisingly, however, due to the love, respect and admiration he had for his parents, he somehow separated them from this unpleasant stereotyping.

After marrying his sweetheart Joyce, it was common knowledge among their friends that Gary was indeed sarcastic. When Gary left home, though he never looked back, it was as if the song, *"Where the Corn Don't Grow,"* performed by Travis Tritt, was written for him. *"As we sat on the front porch of that old grey house where I was born and raised… I said, "Daddy…don't you ever dream about a life where corn don't grow?"* Gary always perceived himself as a professional and continued to pursue a professional career.

As Gary continued to struggle with his feelings, other groups of people became a target for comments and thoughts as well. Where Joyce was not raised with sarcasm and not having an appreciation or understanding of it, she struggled to help Gary see the error of his ways. Joyce is a kind and considerate person and had the patience, not shared by many, to cope with Gary's unique personality.

As you read this, I hope my story does for you what it did for me, as the author.

CHAPTER 1
MOVIN' ON

"You know, someone once said Peter didn't know he could walk on water until he got out of the boat."

"I really don't like desert country," I said to a friend. We were talking about traveling and what it would be like to live in western Idaho. "I would never like to live in country like that. Not much there but sagebrush. About all someone could get out of that area is a good case of Rocky Mountain spotted fever. Or maybe the bite of Diamondback rattler would demand equal time. There's just simply no way I would ever consider living in that country," I declared.

Just then the phone rang.

"It's for you, Gary," someone said.

"Hello?"

"Yeah, Gary, will you come to the office, please?" came a voice over the phone.

"Sure," I responded, a bit confused at the nature of the call. This call seemed strange to me and I felt uneasy.

I immediately went into my supervisor's office where he and my boss were waiting. Upon entering the room, I sensed something was not right, at least for me. I had flashbacks of conversations and announcements where budget cuts were discussed.

Some say it could be intuition or premonition, but nonetheless, I knew something was up.

"Have a seat," my boss said, quietly.

I thought, *maybe someone died or got hurt.* I hate these kinds of scenes because they never turn out well, and I could tell this was not going to be any different.

"We have something we need to tell you," my boss replied in a slow, dry voice. His eyes dropped to the floor as he spoke. However, after the completion of each sentence, he would come up for air and look me in the eye.

"What's that?" I inquired.

"I'll let your supervisor tell you," he replied.

Staring at the floor and with a weak voice, my supervisor approached the discussion. "Gary…"

It seemed like an eternity before he spoke again.

"…with the economy the way it is and the mandatory cuts in the budget, it appears — well, it looks like your salary is not going to be funded in next year's budget."

Remaining confident and really anticipating the bottom line, I inquired, "Oh? What does that mean?"

His voice remained hesitant. "It means, I guess, that we're going to have to let you go."

I sat in silence. I knew what it meant and had even prophesied it to some of my co-workers months prior. It seemed for a few seconds that my life, such as it was, was passing before my eyes. I didn't have seniority in the position I held, so I knew that if budget cuts were to be made I was in the position that would have to go.

At the conclusion of that deafening silence, my boss informed me that I would be unemployed on or before October first. The notification occurred in April of 1980, which would live in infamy. I pondered that phrase for a moment as being too formal for this setting, when you considered that Franklin Delano Roosevelt, a president of the United States, was credited for coining that phrase, probably having been in a far more looming situation than my current position. As hard as this was to bear, I believed good things would come as a result.

So, here I sit in an orange and silver 1977 U-Haul truck, driving down Interstate 84 heading literally into the sunset on my way to a new job, which I am really excited about.

Since no cruise control activator can be found anywhere on the dashboard, I reach over to spin the radio tuner. As I do so, I hear the customary noises typically heard on any AM radio found to be part of the standard equipment in a motor vehicle. The tuner finally falls on what I recognize as a country music station.

"Take this job and shove it..." were the words Johnny Paycheck was emitting from the speaker. *I know that song,* I thought to myself. It's one that's currently being played on the radio and which was sung to me on numerous occasions by one of my fellow employees. He did this after he became aware of my involuntary, pre-scheduled departure from the city. For the past few months, it has often come on the radio in the drafting room where I worked. So my friend, who had nothing but good intentions for my welfare and peace of mind, always took the

opportunity of singing along for my benefit, especially in front of all those within earshot. It was not funny at first, at least until I had secured another job. But knowing I would more than likely do something similar for someone else made me appreciate the humor even more.

As I sat there, with a smile on my face while singing along to the familiar tune, my thoughts fell upon the apostle Peter. *You know,* I thought to myself, *someone once said that Peter didn't know he could walk on water until he got out of the boat.* Peter was encouraged to leave the boat and walk; I, on the other hand, was discharged. So, now that I have been booted from a different vessel, we will see whether I walk or sink. It will all be up to me. As I understand the scripture, Peter was able to walk on water, until his faith waivered. I feel, then, that if I keep my faith strong, I will wander into a profound part of my life.

In order to survive, I guess, I had to convert from rock and roll music to country, as the rock 'n' roll music during the '70s became rather strange to listen to. To me, it never improved, but simply continued on its self-deteriorating path. So, the only rock 'n' roll music I enjoy are some of those that came out in the '50s and '60s.

I notice while I'm driving along a fence line, where the posts are evenly spaced, the effect of the fence posts as I pass by seem to keep time with any music I may be listening to. I also notice the hypnotic effect of the passing fence posts is making me sleepy.

You know, driving these U-Haul trucks isn't so bad. Sitting up high in the truck, as opposed to a car, gives a person a real sense of being in control. Anyway, it is sure a lot less expensive to drive one of these outfits and load it yourself, than it is to hire a moving company.

As I sit in the driver's seat of this well-maintained truck, the center line traffic striping caught my eye as it disappeared beneath the edge of the hood. In leaving my homeland in this rented moving van, I look out the side window and notice the sagebrush move by me. I have observed on many occasions from a moving vehicle how objects, buildings, or trees that are further away seem to pass by more slowly than those up close. Compared to a building a quarter of a mile away, the telephone and fence posts move rapidly. This phenomenon, coupled with the steady hum of a partially worn-out V-8 engine mounted under the hood in front of me, cause my mind to wander. Usually, depending on my mood, my thoughts will go either all positive or all negative. I think the latter is where I'm headed.

Since losing my job, I have felt wounded and hurt. While understanding I was not let go due to performance issues, but rather as a result of a budget cutback, try as I might I have not yet been able to remove the unkind feelings I have harbored for my boss. My perception is that since we did not see eye-to-eye often, the fact I have departed his department likely causes him some joy. So from my perspective, it seemed he was the type of person who didn't want anyone around him, myself included, to advance. For me he did not promote extra schooling and did not approve of me working my way up through the ranks of his department the way I had. I was a project manager, and as such assumed quite a bit of technical responsibility. I often felt he would make sure I wasn't given credit for things I achieved, and tried to minimize the significance of the position I had attained.

I have never understood why people have that insecurity. If I were a supervisor working with a big corporation and had five employees with PhDs while my education consisted of a lesser amount, and I would utilize their talents to promote them, ultimately we all could achieve greater success. If, on the other hand, I were to have a PhD and supervised six people with Bachelor of Science degrees, were I to spend my time belittling

21

and dragging them down, productivity would eventually decline and they may do things to undermine me. There is, in some respect, an eternal principle here: Our Heavenly Father has children, places them on an earth; teaches them truth, allows them to be exposed to evil, and gives them ways to get through trials. If they are true to His teachings, by overcoming the evil and trials that face them, they hopefully choose the life He has prepared for them.

I caught myself trying to convince an invisible audience somewhere in this moving van if we simply treat everyone the way we would like to be treated, in most case our management skills and successfulness in business would be greatly enhanced.

Anyway, it was okay that my boss felt the way he did; after all, he didn't hire me to be a project manager, which was where I had finally arrived. Instead, I hired on to be an engineering technician. There was nothing wrong with that. The whole problem was simply, in my opinion, after working for about one year I realized I wanted to advance past the engineering tech position.

Well, I have done just that. I have been hired to be the City Engineer of a small town and am I excited! Yes, we can get rewarded for our efforts, and I am here to say good things do come to those who wait.

After being notified of my employment status, I have had much time to ponder and think, and during this humbling and stressful time it soon became obvious to me had I not been laid off, I would likely not have pursued the job for which I was just hired. Seldom are life's lessons realized when things are going well.

CHAPTER 2
HANK

24

"I'll show those farmers that I can get a real job in the city where there is culture and stuff."

This interstate highway is certainly boring to pass over, especially considering I have never enjoyed traveling in a vehicle to begin with. It annoys me when I just want to be some place and have to go through this process of traveling in order to get anywhere. People make such a fuss over seeing the countryside. "Did you see the 'Blues' last month, weren't they pretty, with all the snow just starting to melt?" Or, "isn't that a great drive over the Lost Trail Pass. Wow!" Yes, they are attractive, but I grew up in that country and have seen it all. Sometimes I think people making those comments don't even care about the scenery, but just enjoy being a part of the conversation.

For me personally, I would just as well be at one place or another, but don't expect me to be excited about "seeing the country." When I was a kid, my family would go to Idaho from Montana, about a five hour drive, and the best trip I had was when I slept the whole way without waking up. *That* was wonderful.

I have viewed enough of the earth to have a pretty good idea of what it looks like, and so far I've not been overly excited upon discovering new landmarks. I can honestly say I don't get a buzz like some people in seeing the sights. I more so appreciate the destination than the process of the journey. In fact, if it weren't for the crying and whining of my children combined with the gentle persuasion of my wife, we would not stop anywhere except when we needed refueling.

I've often thought about the aircraft used by the Air Force to refuel fighter jets and other aircraft in flight. I have been trying to scheme a way to modify my car so I can put extra fuel tanks in the trunk, thereby allowing me, with the assistance of some ingenuity, to top off my fuel tank "in flight." This would allow me to extend my range and reduce the amount of travel time required for the trip. I do not have my wife's approval for this — yet.

Now I get how some people really enjoy traveling and seeing the sights. Just looking out across this place — all I see is desert. Everything's here but the cactus. I'll betcha there are even some scorpions out here. In coming to this high desert country, it's a good thing I know what to expect. You see, I grew up in western Montana where the mountains are high enough to support snow well into the summer months; where there are trees in the mountains that a person can really get some shade from, and where there is a river called the Bitterroot, which keeps the humidity up and the country side green, unlike this place.

I suppose that begs the question, if this area is so uninviting, why am I here? From my limited understanding at a young age, I have to say the reason I didn't stay back in Montana is there's not much in the way of a promising career for a young man trying to make a start in life.

Farming's a lifestyle of which I have long detested in that homeland of mine. It was repeatedly manifested at the old grocery store, where I would go after football practice to call my mom for a ride home. The store was situated across the street from the high school, so it was easy access when you needed a snack or a cold drink. On the north end of the store, which was approximately 40 feet long and 10 feet wide, sat a drugstore bar where you could eat or drink coffee, which was the beverage of choice for the adults frequenting there. The bar hosted four or five stools and ran perpendicular to the length of the building.

On the bar was an old stitched leather dice shaker, which probably came west with the first wagon train when someone had the foresight to settle this area. The bottom half of the shaker was kind of a shiny black color, which I surmised came from all those dice enchanted farmers fondling it for all those years. Working with cattle and all, one can only imagine where their hands have been. Apparently the farmers felt some type of relaxation after chasing cows through the neighbor's yard and bucking hay bales all day.

Further to the right side of the counter laid a small device, about three inches wide and eight inches long, which had several symmetrically placed dimples in it. Lying near it was a little object that resembled a key one would use to open a sardine can. To operate it, a player would use the key to push out a folded piece of paper which had a number written on it. If you got the right number, you would win a prize.

While playing with the game pieces once, I was dutifully informed that it was a *punch board,* and that I was too young to use it. Gambling! They couldn't fool me even though I was just a youngster. I don't know if gambling was legal or not in Montana back then, but they seemed to have legalized the punch board themselves anyway. It appeared if you were to buy a punch for a dime, it would be your good fortune to win a seven-and-one half inch piece of beef jerky and two "hands off" dances with a real nice (semiconscious) barmaid at the local tavern. What a cultural experience! The only occasion I had to be in a bar for any significant time, other than to use the phone, was when I snuck in, underage, and played the drums for a couple of hours.

That cost me a few strokes because my dad had been looking for me all over town, and finally found me there.

Closer to the edge of the counter, in a kind of disarray, sat some old, unwashed coffee mugs that appeared to have never been washed after the first use. It looked like there was about 1/16 inch of age-hardened sediment in the bottom of each cup. Interesting habits these people have.

Sometimes I would sit for as much as an hour waiting for Mom to come get me. During that time I would talk to the store owner, who everybody referred to as "Colonel," because he had military memorabilia hung all over his store. If there was a longer story to his military past, I hadn't been privy to it. He would ask me how football was going and talk about sports in a clumsy conversation that wasn't important to either one of us. I remember when I would go trick-or-treating on Halloween night, even as seniors in high school without wearing a mask, he would give us a big Baby Ruth or Butterfinger candy bar. I guess I really didn't relate to him, but liked being around him, nonetheless.

I would sit there waiting with him staring at me, hoping something would happen to break the boredom. I was never really sure whether the Colonel was just being friendly or if he suspected I might be a shoplifter, giving him an excuse to hang around until my ride came.

Then it would happen. At about 5:30 in the afternoon, starved of a cultural experience and needin' a fix, a farmer would usually drive up to the store in some kind of pickup; either rebuilt, homebuilt, or just as is, but seldom a new one. If it was new, it was usually trashed inside of two years. I was always perturbed when a farmer would get a new pickup, and then turn right around loading it up with heavy cow manure until the frame was sittin' on the axle, then head off on a bumpy old road at 40 or 50 miles an hour. It wasn't fair. Here I have wanted a nice, new pickup ever since I can remember, but all I could have was an old, mostly worn-out 1966 Chevy that someone overloaded with wet concrete.

The farm truck windows were kinda dirty most likely because they had never been washed. There was some noticeable dried cow manure on the back window from when they took the steer to be butchered six months earlier, and the animal leaned against the front stock rack and relieved itself on the cab. There was the remaining part of a bale of hay in the back of the pickup, with a pitch fork stuck in it, which appears to have been there for months. In these parts, many would substitute a red or blue handkerchief (since I believe they were the only colors available) for a recently misplaced gas cap. It seemed functional, but I always wondered what would happen if a full tank of gas would slosh around and get the bottom of the handkerchief wet and create the perfect Molotov cocktail-on-wheels for some pyromaniac passing by, looking for a thrill. As I believed farmers were oblivious to any culture or sophistication, home-made gas caps drew little attention from anyone else.

After parking askew to the other parking places, he would shut the engine off. Usually due to the lack of the engine being in proper time, the engine would "diesel" for a few seconds and finally quit, followed by a loud report, creating a small plume of smoke that would fill the air in the immediate vicinity with exhaust fumes.

As I watch the driver push on the door a few times because the hinge mechanism has never been lubricated, he slowly gets out of the pickup. The door would make a loud popping sound and finally open. He would step out of the pickup, stretch, and look up and down the street. He would then take a deep breath and slowly walk up the steps, open the screen door and enter the store. This ritual would happen every day at the same appointed time. Whether or not he had more pressing matters, he would be there.

The farmers always wore the same old, blue coveralls, which stink of cow manure. Depending on a number of reasons, I suppose, a suspender was left off of the shoulder, causing me to wonder why it wasn't removed, rather than allowing it to hang down and get in the way of the pocket. Sometimes a shirt was worn, other times, not. To accent the dress of the day, the men usually wore some old, laced boots with a matching hat, which had a sweat band that is all soaked and gross. I think one can determine the age of a farmers hat, taking into consideration how far the sweat has moved up his hat and across the brim. The ensemble was never complete without a piece of grass or a cigarette hangin' out of his mouth. If he had been working in the hay, there would be small pieces of hay leaves all over his hat and face, but it didn't seem to bother him. I recall on many occasions myself, reaching down to grab a piece of grass or hay and put it in my mouth when out in the field. Obvious to me, had I not escaped, that culture would have entrapped me and I may never have recovered from it.

After entering the store, he would find his self-assigned stool, look around, and sit down. Unless someone else sat in it first, the farmers always sat on the same stool every day. A hat might be left on, while others would take theirs off and set it on the counter. Removing their hats would always expose the fact their white, shiny heads had little or no contact with any photons from the sun.

Never saw a farmer that didn't wear a hat. The older farmers would usually wear a hat with a round brim, like a straw hat. The younger ones — and they all looked like dinosaurs to me when I was a kid — wore a hat with a bill. They would wear their hats tipped to the left side of their head somewhere between 20 to 35 degrees from the vertical axis. Some of the real sharp farmers would flip their bill up in front. I would always laugh whenever I saw one wearing his hat with the bill flipped up that way. I guess this is about the only thing a farmer could remotely relate to as being in style.

You ought to go swimming when there are farmers in the pool. They have a white upper torso, a leathery red face (especially the smokers, and most of them were); a bright red burn on the top of their chest forming a triangle caused from leaving the top button of their shirts undone, and a deep tan on their hands and arms, up to their elbows. The rest of their bodies looked like a jar full of mayonnaise. It was a great site for all to behold. Among other stimulating events, a typical conversation would go something like this:

Speaking to me in a friendly, monotone voice, "How are ya, Son?"

"Fine." I responded in kind.

"How's yer dad doing? Haven't seen him for quite a while, now. I guess he's probably pretty busy gettin' those spuds in."

It irritated me when people asked questions and then went right on answering them. It usually made for a short and meaningless conversation.

"He's pretty busy, alright," trying to ante up his question.

"Say, you sure looked good the other day when you ran that hundred yard dash, or whatever it was. I thought it was real exceptional that Corvallis was able to beat Loyola." His neck must have been stiff, by the way he craned to look at me while he spoke.

"It was one of the best races I have ever run," I said, confidently.

Loyola High School was located in Missoula, a town of nearly 40,000 people, located about 50 miles north of Corvallis, and was a Catholic School for boys. While the student bodies of both schools were similar in size, theirs consisted of all boys, while our student body was composed of boys and girls. I didn't mind, as girls are nice to have around. When it came to competition, they had almost twice the number of boys to pick from than did we. With that, the deck was always stacked against us, so it was special when we beat them; not only for the sport participants, but the farmers as well. You have to understand that over 50 percent of the spectators were farmers.

"What do ya think, Son? Are ya figgerin' on going to one of them there colleges and playin' sports after you get out of high school? I suspect that would be a good deal for ya if'n you could do 'er. You seem to be a pretty good athlete." He rounded out his comment with a squint and a smile.

I thought I was too, but it was sure nice hearing it from someone else. This farmer always attended the games no matter whether his kids were playing or not. So I figured he had to know something about sports.

Before I answered, he continued. "I'd have liked to play some football in college, but I had to quit school 'fore the 8th grade to work on the farm. Seems like I always had somethin' agin' me whenever I have tried to do somethin' I wanted to do," he muttered.

The farmer sat there on the bar stool for several minutes in silence, fumbling with the dice shaker and looking down at the counter.

"Son," he finally said, "ya know, you got it a lot easier than I did when I was tryin' to grow up. Yep, we didn't have the time to

32

be gettin' into mischief like you kids do now. We had to be in school, or we had better be out takin' care of those livestock and gettin' the crops in. And another thing, I don't remember havin' any of them fancy machines to work with like you kids do now. It seems to me, whether you kids are workin' or playin', it's still just playin'. I don't know what this world is comin' to." The farmer set his coffee cup down and shook his head loosely.

In my young mind, I didn't understand why farmers had to look the way they did. They didn't seem to care what type of image they projected to other people. It amazed me they had a wife that loved and supported them. From what I could tell, for the most part, they all had wives. Seemed to me they couldn't function at the level they did and run the farm if it weren't for their wives. Surprisingly enough, some of their wives were very classy ladies; some of them took good care of themselves.

"I guess it's okay you didn't go to college. You seem to be doing alright on the farm. You're getting along okay, aren't you?" I finally asked, not really caring about the answer.

I really shouldn't have been so phony, but I felt sorry for him; he seemed so sincere. It really did look to me like he needed something, some type of sophistication. Hardly looked like he could produce enough money to buy a steak, much less spend three or four thousand dollars for a herd of calves at the drop of a hat. I just didn't know how those farmers did it.

"How the heck ya doin', Hank?" came a voice through the back door of the store. The back door connected the store to an apartment where the store owner lived. He must have heard the farmer's voice.

"I guess I can't complain. I'm still kickin'," came the response.

"So, what ya been doing today?" the Colonel inquired.

"Well, I'm kinda tearin' up my machinery, I guess."

"Oh, how's that?"

"Well, you know how it is when yer drivin' one of them there swathers into the sun. I was going along there when one of them rooster pheasants flew up in front of me. I was lookin' real close to see if I'd cut his legs off, 'cause he flew up so close to the mower knife. About that time I done drove the swather right into the fence by the canal there and got the barbwire all tangled up in the reel. So, I spent most of the day just tryin' to get the broke reel untangled and replaced." He continued the play-by-play. "What really made it a hassle is the fact that I was clear out away from the house and I didn't have my tools, except for an old crescent wrench and a bent flat blade screw driver. Them ain't tools to be fixin' no reel, if ya know what I mean."

The Colonel nodded with an intense interest; apparently he *did* know what the farmer meant.

"I'd like t'blowed my lungs out trying to call the ol' lady so she could bring my pickup over with the tools. She couldn't hear me," Hank grunted the last words.

I hate it when the farmers refer to their wives as old ladies. It seems like they don't have any more respect for their wives than they do an old sow pig. The irony — a word I learned in high school English class that I'm guessing farmers don't know about — of the whole thing is that the wives have a lot more class than those farmers do that refer to them as old ladies. Some said it was a sign of love, but I found it disrespectful.

"Can ya believe it?" Hank said, "Yep, I had to walk the whole

34

way back to the house, which is about a quarter of a mile, as you know. When I got there, I knew the ol' lady had taken the car to town, with my keys in it so I couldn't get into the tool box. So, I suspect it don't take much figgerin' for you to see I had to scrounge some other tools, and it took the whole day to get that reel fixed and back onto the swather." I caught myself staring at Hank as he spoke.

"How do you like yer coffee, Hank?" asked the Colonel, switching conversation gears.

"Black as the ace of spades," Hank replied, winking at me.

I have always been amused at the sayings our society has placed upon us. Seems like we never get tired of them — no matter how ridiculous they sound.

"How about you, Son?" It took a moment for me to realize the Colonel was inquiring as to my preference.

"I...I don't drink it," I said with some embarrassment, know-ing in that little social circle you had to drink coffee, among other things, in order to be a "man." *Besides,* I thought to myself, *look what it has done to these people.*

"Hank, where did ya get all that alfalfa in yer hair? Were ya showing one of those young things where the hay stack was?" the Colonel said, with a bellowing laugh.

"Na. As a matter of fact there's a hole in the window of my swather," the farmer explained. *Of course there is,* I thought to myself.

"Did ya fall asleep and break it with yer head?" the store own-er asked, with a grin and another wink.

35

Hank was kinda slow to respond. "Ya wanna know what happened?"

The store owner nodded; I rolled my eyes.

"I was running that there new swather I bought this spring along the old ditch I used to use for floodin' the place, ya know? I had plumb fergot about that shallow trench that came out from the ditch. I was gonna fill 'er in last fall before I got the new sprinkler system put in, but I never got 'round to it. Anyway, all of a sudden the wheel of the swather dropped into the trench, there, and really stirred things up. I had the old 12 gauge right next to me in the cab in case I saw one of them rooster pheasants. So, when I hit the trench, the gun flipped down and hit the steering wheel hard enough to go off. It musta been cheap glass, 'cause it done blowed a hole right in the middle of my windshield!"

The Colonel chuckled. "Is that what messed yer hat all up there, Hank?"

"Yep, you sure got it right there. I plumb fergot ta tell ya that when I hit the trench there, the swather liked t'buck me right out of my seat and I hit my head on the roof. It's sure a good thing I didn't get knocked out or the swather might be trying to climb up the side of the ol' chicken coop by now!" Hank looked down for a few seconds, then spoke again, "I guess the ol' lady didn't inspect me very well this mornin' when I was a-puttin' on my duds. Looks like I done left my zipper down again."

"Pays to advertise," the Colonel said, still chuckling.

Yes, they really do have a sense of humor, I thought to myself. It's not very well refined, but they nonetheless have one. That does surprise me because I always thought older people didn't have a sense of humor. I always assumed that it took all they had just to make a living and that life was just a pain, at best. It seemed that whenever they did laugh, it was at things that weren't very funny. This seemed different.

"Yep, I keep on tryin' but it doesn't seem to do any good. The women just don't seem to have any use for me," Hank replied.

They better not, I thought; *you're married!* Then I pondered that perhaps if he didn't refer to his wife as the "ol' lady," maybe things would be different. I don't think these old boys have much of an understanding as to how to deal with women. All they're worried about is working till dark and "eatin' meat, taters and gravy." I swear, if they didn't get their meat, taters and gravy every day, for every meal, they would have exploded. I supposed they did actually eat something different for breakfast. I wondered if they have ever eaten pizza, or maybe a taco. I'll bet that was a disgusting thought to them. Maybe the women would like to go out and have some different food — and this may be pushing it — some shrimp or something; not meat, taters and gravy, and something they didn't have to cook.

Just then the screen door opened, and in walked the sheriff. "Hi guys," he said. My attention shifted to watching the confidence he walked in with. He made sure to stand in the doorway and let the screen door gently close, rather than allowing it to slam.

"Whatcha doin' clear out here? Are ya lost or did ya just have to get out of the office?" Hank inquired.

He's the Sheriff, I thought. *Why don't they show him some respect?* He's way more professional than they will ever be, and he is pretty popular here, too. If anybody is going to be disrespectful, it should be a teenager like me, not a stupid farmer — someone you would refer to as an adult, anyway.

I have always had respect for the police; in fact, that last summer I worked for one. I was never completely comfortable around him, but I always respected him.

"No," responded the Sheriff, and gave a polite chuckle. "Actually, I'm out here checking on some more reports of cows being killed for some of their organs."

"Maybe you should check out old Hank, here. He loves those beef hearts," the Colonel said with a laugh.

"Can't blame him," the sheriff said with a smile. "No, some kind of cult or religious thing, I guess. You know, people aren't above anything, anymore." He accepted a cup of coffee before continuing. "While I'm here, I wanted to ask if you've seen anything suspicious going on near the old Hawkins Ranch? There were five head of Holstein cows found dead last night, with their hearts and livers cut out."

"Sheriff, I haven't seen a thing," said Hank, with all the sincerity he could muster.

"Well, thanks, boys. Be sure to let me know if you come across anything," the sheriff said, reaching into his pocket for a loose dollar bill to cover the coffee. The Colonel put his hand up and said, "On the house, Sheriff." The sheriff touched the brim of his hat as he opened the door and stepped out, again preventing the screen door from slamming.

"See ya down the road," Hank said, waving a hand in the air.

"I really hate to see this place get ruined by those outsiders. Look how they're screwing up everything. We gotta start lockin' up everything now. A man just can't trust anybody, anymore." The Colonel was mad. The vein on his forehead was more prominent than usual, and I couldn't help but stare at it for a moment.

I could hear the sound of a John Deere tractor coming up the street and then the engine was shut off. I always liked the sound of those tractors. I had spent many hours mowing hay on one.

Several minutes later there was a long, loud honk of a horn. Then we heard, "Why don't ya try yer lights? Yer horn works."

"What's all the commotion about?" Hank asked, rising up an inch from his seat.

"Let me see." The Colonel walked over to the window and peered out for several seconds.

Someone else yelled from outside, my guess was from inside the honking car. "Get that piece of junk out of the street so a person can drive through here!"

"You won't believe this," the Colonel began. "Zeb Jackson has got his John Deere tractor parked out in the street, changing his oil."

We all rushed to the door and went outside. It was a funny scenario. There in the street next to the service station was parked Zeb's tractor all right, with oil dripping into an oil pan beneath. The funny part to me was the partially-emptied manure spreader hooked to the tractor, setting in the hot sun, and it was *ripe*.

The guy in the car was still honkin' his horn. He had one of those big four-door Lincoln Continental convertibles. The driver himself was a tall, overweight guy you could just tell was from the "big city." He had on a white shirt and tie; looked like he was pretty rich, too.

Rich people were interesting to me to watch. They seemed to be just a little better than the rest; in their minds, at least. I remember on one occasion going to the bank with my dad to meet with the banker. When we got there, we stood chatting with him on the street. He was dressed as though he thought he was a real cowboy, although he was probably a "drugstore" cowboy, purchasing the garb he thought would offer the right persona. With the way he talked and strutted around, I think he was convinced that he was legendary. It reminds me of a proverb in the Bible:

> *"Put not forth thyself in the presence of the king, and stand not in the place of great men; For better it is that it be said unto thee, Come up hither; than that thou shouldest be put lower in the presence of the prince whom thine eyes have seen." Proverbs 25:6-7*

My interpretation of this was metaphorical. When you go to the banquet of life, you don't sit at the head table. Instead, you sit in the audience until you are invited to come up. Otherwise, if you are told you are not supposed to be at the head table and, instead, are asked to sit in the audience, you will have lost your credibility with anyone who witnessed the event, and you may never get it back. The banker lost his credibility with me when he put himself up to be so important, when, in reality, he was not.

My dad owed him some money — well, actually not him, but the bank. I think Dad gave him a payment or something. The banker said, "That should be enough for supper." By his laughter, I believed he thought he was being funny. I thought it was a very ignorant comment for him to be making to my dad. I wasn't very old at the time, but it has stayed with me.

The guy in the car seemed to resemble the mindset of the banker.

Zeb wasn't about to back down. "Why don't you shut that horn

off, before I unload this manure on that land yacht of yer's?"

"If you don't move that tractor this instant, I'm going to have to report this to the sheriff," the driver warned.

The Colonel yelled at the driver. "Why don't you just go around him and stop all this fuss?"

Hank chimed in, "I don't want to disappoint you, sir, but the sheriff is this guy's brother." I couldn't help but laugh.

Another wink from the Colonel.

After sitting there for a few minutes, the driver finally pushed the gas pedal to the floor, sped around the tractor, and left. Even though it was funny, I still didn't think it was right for the farmers to treat the driver that way. He wasn't trying to bother anybody. Sometimes these farmers just don't seem to get it.

Zeb walked across the street to where we were standing, a big grin sliding across his face. "He's going pretty fast. Maybe I should report him. I got this license number." Zeb produced an oily piece of paper with numbers scrawled on it.

"I think you've already caused enough trouble, Zeb. You know it's not right to park a vehicle in the street like that," the Colonel chided.

"I know. But I didn't want to unhook the spreader and I couldn't get the tractor off the street," was Zeb's explanation.

"So, how've ya been, Zeb? Haven't seen ya for quite a spell," the Colonel inquired, slapping Zeb on the shoulder.

"I've been pretty busy," Zeb replied.

"Oh? You've actually been doing something?" the store owner asked, his sarcasm dripping.

Zeb began his explanation. "Ya. I've been over helping Jack Anderson for the last few days. He was pickin' apples the other day, and if you know Jack, he never quits until the job is done, whether he can do it or not."

"I know what ya mean," Hank nodded in agreement.

"Anyway," Zeb continued, "he was at the top of the tree there, and was reachin' for the last apple, when the ladder slipped. You shoulda heard his ol' lady. She started screamin' at 'im and carryin' on. It was funny."

"Was he hurt?" I asked, a bit annoyed with Zeb's sense of humor.

"A little. His leg got caught on a branch and he twisted his knee when he fell. I've been helpin' him with his flood irrigatin'."

It was interesting to watch Zeb talk. He blinked his left eye all the time, to the point it could become annoying to whomever he was talking. His left hand was kinda messed up from when he was putting in fence posts; I guess one time he placed it on top of the post, and the post hammer came down and hit it. Can you imagine, leaving your hand on top of a post while you use your other hand to activate the post hammer that smashes your hand? I was incredulous with how these farmers can be. It was obvious they were totally oblivious to how they came across to other people.

After a minute or two had passed, Hank said, "Zeb, I heard you washed out the road up there by that there old silo, next to John Hill's ranch, and the fur was 'bout to fly. Can ya tell us a little more about it, there?"

The Colonel looked at me with a grin and everything got quiet. I guess Zeb didn't want to talk about "that there subject" very much.

"Come on, Zeb, tell us about it," the Colonel persuaded.

"Ok, if ya have to know everything," Zeb said, and began with a heavy sigh. "I was headin' down the road and all a'sudden I heard this real loud whistle. I looked in my rear view mirror and there was this real nice-looking girl in a swimmin' suit, ridin' horseback an' whistling to her dog. I was sorta checkin' her out when my right front wheel moved onto the shoulder of the road. The dang shoulder was soft, and it pulled my pickup right into the check and broke the boards in the head gate; and, well...the water started to run everywhere."

"That ain't the whole story, there, Zeb," Hank blurted out.

With some embarrassment, Zeb finally said, "Not everyone knows this so please don't go tellin' anyone else." He paused for a moment. "We had to call the fire department out to sandbag the canal so the water would stop floodin' John's beets."

"Can't be starin' at those women, Zeb; it'll get you in trouble every time," the Colonel scolded as he laughed.

After everyone finished shaking their heads and making all the usual comments that accompanies an ordeal like this, we went back into the store.

"Well, Son," Hank blurted out, "maybe you oughta be a farmer instead of going to college. Maybe you could have as much fun as I've had today." He gripped my shoulder and shook it slightly.

43

"I don't think so," I replied, with no uncertainty, hoping he caught my indignant tone.

No way would I ever be a farmer, I thought. Just look at these guys. Who in their right mind or with any mind at all would want to be a farmer? Especially when you have 17 years of forewarning as to what it would be like.

My reminiscing as I drove the U-Haul continued for a moment longer. I remembered sometime back, after this kid I knew had graduated ahead of me from high school; I would see him hanging out at the grocery store with the farmers. Then one day he came to the store, wearing those coveralls. I thought to myself, *Oh, no, they've got him. He's allowed those farmers to get him. Now they'll screw his mind up and he will be lost forever.* I knew, then, that I needed to get the heck out of there, and soon. I'd show those farmers I could get a real job in the city, where there was culture and stuff.

//

CHAPTER 3
THE DAM

//

46

"Remember in the Bible when the Lord said if we don't keep His com-mandments, we will be damned?"

Now you know why I'm cruising into this desert, pursuing a real career. Surely there is more to life than being a farmer.

"Dad, what are all those pipes out there spraying the water for?" my son, Brad, asked. He begged me to let him ride along in the truck to our new destination.

"Those are sprinklers, Son. They try to trick the plants into thinking there is rain coming down on them." *I am so clever,* I thought to myself. My wife says I joke too much with the kids; she's afraid they won't take me seriously when they get older.

"No sir, Dad. They don't trick the plants." Maybe she's right; he doesn't seem to believe me now.

"You see that little house down by the river?" I started, changing the subject a little. "You are gonna have to look fast or you'll miss it. Can you see it? It's... right...there!" I pointed to help him spot the home.

"Ya." he replied, sitting a bit straighter.

47

"That's what they call a pump house. There is a large pump inside that pumps water from the river into that big pipeline over there. From there it goes into smaller pipes that have the sprinklers on them. Do you understand what I'm saying?"

"Ya. That's what makes our food grow, huh, Dad," more a statement than a question.

"Where did you hear that?" I inquired.

"We learned it in school last week. My teacher says it's called 'irrigation.' We also learned that if there wasn't any irrigation, the land would be a desert."

Boy, isn't that the truth, I thought. This desolate hole would be worthless without those sprinklers.

"What's that guy doing over there?" Brad asked, pointing to a man attempting to handle the pipes alone. ·

"He's changing the sprinkler pipes. Doesn't that look fun?" I asked.

"No way," he answered, wrinkling his nose a bit.

"You're right, Son, it's not a lot of fun. But it sure teaches ya how to work." I wrinkled *my* nose after hearing my words. I hated it when Dad would tell me that. Workin' on the farm was pretty hard. I guess my dad was just trying to teach me something. But I sure couldn't see it at the time. Ya know, it reminds me of when my dad taught me to flood irrigate. An experience I will never forget. My mind rolled back in time.

"Gary, bring me that shovel that's in the back of the pick-up."

48

"This one?" I asked, not wanting to disappoint.

"No, Son, the one that is round on the end. We can't do much irrigating with a square-nosed shovel."

"Why not?"

"Bring it over here and I'll show you." My dad was always great at answering my questions, no matter how mundane or repetitive. "Now, take this and try to dig up that thistle. Not like that. Let me take it." I handed him the shovel and he began to demonstrate. "Put your foot on it like this and then push your weight down on it."

"Show me," I said, again, not wanting to look poorly in front of my father.

"No, I want you to try it on your own," came his reply. He was never rude in his instruction, but rather very direct.

"Like this?" I tried to push the square-nosed shovel into the hard dirt.

"Yes, just like that."

"It's not doing anything. How are you supposed to do it, Dad?"

"Here, Son, now take this shovel and try it." He switched implements and handed me the round-nosed shovel.

"I see," I said, as I stepped on the shovel. "This shovel is a lot easier. What is a square nose shovel for, Dad?"

"To make kids ask questions." I caught the glint in his eye.

"No sir, Dad. Tell me the truth."

"Do you remember that trough in the floor of the barn behind where the cows stand when we are milking them?"

"Ya," I answered.

"A square-nosed shovel works pretty well for cleaning the manure out."

"Gross."

"You asked."

"Ya, I did."

"Okay, Son, you see here where the water has stopped running and the ground is dry?"

"Ya."

"What we have to do is move this dam up here, so we can give the grass right here a drink," he instructed.

"Dad, did you just swear?" I could feel my eyes open wide.

"No, Son."

"I thought you said da...uh..." I began, but didn't want to be disrespectful.

"I did," he answered with a nod.

"Isn't that swearing?"

"No. Not this time. That's what it's really called. Remember in the Bible when the Lord said if we don't keep His commandments we will be damned?"

"Ya."

"That kind of damn and this kind of dam are spelled differently, but they mean the same thing. They both mean you are going to be stopped," my dad explained, smiling.

"Oh," I said, realizing I have learned something. My dad seemed to be pretty smart.

"Okay, Son, what we have to do is lift up on this edge of the dam and let the water run under it. I'll do it on this side of the ditch and you do it on that side," he said as he directed me with his hands. We have to hurry, now, so we can get the dam set over there before the water reaches us. If we can beat the water, it's a lot easier. After we lift up the edges, we have to grab both ends of this pole and hurry as quickly as we can." He looked me square in the eyes. "Are ya ready?"

"Ya."

"Okay. Pull it up. That's it."

"Look at the water run, Dad! Oh, look, the dam is floating away!" I squealed, sure I had done something wrong.

"It'll be alright. Just grab the pole. Have ya got it?" He didn't seem mad.

"Ya."

"Okay, let's go."

51

"Looks like we're gonna beat the water!" I said, proud I had noticed.

"Yep. Be careful so you don't trip. Okay, put the pole down right here. Ya, like that. Grab that other corner and pull it tight like this. See what I'm doing?" he explained.

"Ya."

"Okay, put your foot on it and be careful that you don't slip."

"Look, Dad, the water is coming!"

"Don't worry, it'll work okay," he assured me. "Okay, Son, see how I am pushing the middle of the dam down?"

"Ya."

"Now, watch the water fill 'er up." I did just as he said.

"That's neat. Look at that frog swimming there."

"Ya, we kinda messed up his home didn't we? Okay, Son, now we have to cut some holes into the bank here, to let the water out."

"What about those other holes? Shouldn't we fill those in first?" I was a bit surprised at my own vested interest.

"No, Son, if we do that, the water won't have any place to go and it will flood over and wash out the whole ditch bank. Then you will get to see just how fast you can work that round-nosed shovel."

"I see," but didn't know if I truly did.

"Isn't irrigating fun?" he asked.

52

"Ya, I want to do it when I grow up!" I would remember those words in days to come.

"I hope you don't have to," my dad said under his breath. Those words would also come back to me. My dad is a great guy. I have learned a lot from him. When I was growing up, he did things for a lot of people. I admired his servitude, but didn't really grasp why he was so willing.

Sometime later, my brother and I got a job changing sprinklers. We thought it was a real good deal. After all, we could make $10.00 per week. Look at all that big money. I always wanted a motorcycle, so I guess I thought any money to be put towards a motorcycle was good money.

Several weeks went by with my brother and me changing them together. We would move the pipes from one side of the property to the other. It took about one week to cover the ground. As we got close to the middle of the season, we started getting frustrated because of those sprinklers. We had to move them every day and usually in tall wet grass, around buildings, through and over fences and swampy ground. At the end of the week we luckily got a day off while the farmer we were working for moved them back to the other end of the property.

These sprinklers were really old, the pipes were bent, and sometimes the valve wouldn't shut off right. On many occasions, as best as I can recollect, after working in the cold and wet, and finally finishing a line, as we were waiting for the pipe to fill up we'd hear a loud gushing sound and knew the line had separated. After getting very tired of all that, we schemed about how we would find another job so that we could quit this one. We did find another job, however, Mom wouldn't let us quit our sprinkler job, and to make things really frustrating, she made us work our second job, as well. We were able to make a little mon-

ey, but was that hard work. I don't ever want to change sprinklers again, as long as I live.

///

CHAPTER 4
THE BUM

///

"There are a lot of God's children that wear ponytails, and I am sure He loves them too..."

"**D**ad," a voice came from a small figure lying on the seat, who had just awakened from a nap. "Are we there yet?" Brad blurted out in a semi-conscious state, while rubbing his eyes and looking out the window.

How many times I have listened to that question. It must be a centuries-old statement, back to the days when pioneers had wagons, or even when the family just walked. The impatience of youth must span the time from when the first human family decided to travel to the present; not that I blame them for those uninvited outbursts, as I still struggle with the monotony of travel, myself. I recall using that phrase on a number of occasions as a frustrated passenger. I don't recollect the total blame for my impatience was placed squarely upon the monotony of the journey, but rather the anticipation of seeing my cousin, Grandma, and Grandpa. I believe they were the ones who took the leading role. That expression of anxiety, which was usually developed from the back seat of any family car, has been perpetuated into the adult world as well.

Brad is my oldest son. He begged to ride with me while our other children — Nick, Karen, and Melissa — chose to ride with their mother and would be coming along later.

"No, I don't think so. We have a couple more hours to go yet,

Son. Isn't this a pretty drive?" I asked, somewhat sarcastically. I'm pretty sure when someone look up the word sarcasm in the dictionary, they would find a picture of my smirking face. I laced my commentaries with sarcasm quite frequently, and wasn't altogether sure Brad had picked up my tone.

"Yuck," was the reply with conviction, from a very observant and confident young man.

"Just look at all of this pretty country, Son. I don't think it gets any better than this. Just look at the sagebrush and those rocks." I waved my hand over the dashboard, certain my son would pick up on my tone this time.

I really was concerned about the sagebrush. Doctors say you can get ticks from the bushes, and on some occasions, the ticks have Lyme disease. Apparently, Lyme disease introduces bacteria into the body, and if left untreated is nearly impossible to cure. It is interesting to note about sagebrush that wherever it elects to put down its roots, other plants will not thrive.

Another gripe I have with the desert: it's not so exciting when you look down the freeway and see a mirage. I thought to myself, *a person would have to be just a little crazy to want to fight very hard to protect this place.* But, then, I knew it just wasn't the landscape I preferred.

"Dad, look at that guy walkin' there." Brad said, then asked, "Why does he look so bad?" He took a brief glance at me before turning back.

He really *didn't* look very well, at all. He looked as though he had dressed himself in flea market throw-aways. Unless it has something to do with how people feel about themselves, it makes no sense why they dress that way. Anyone can look clean and neat in inexpensive clothes, or those you can find at a garage or rummage

sale, even a second hand store.

"I don't know why he looks that way, Son," I answered, speaking honestly and trying to avoid sounding judgmental.

This man looked real mean, too, like someone you would never want to pick up if he were hitchhiking. With all the stories ya hear, I sometimes feel guilty about not picking up people like that. My philosophy about picking up hitchhikers is that if I get a real strong feeling I need to pull over, then I do it. If not, I continue on my way, as I am doing now. I have had inclinations to stop and pick people up before, so it's not just a line I use to feel better.   We were given a brain to judge whether or not it is the correct thing to do when scary situations arise. I don't think God expects us to always be a "Good Samaritan" to a rattle snake, if we perceive there is a good chance it's going to strike. Anyway, there were no warm fuzzy feelings in my heart about stopping now.

His hair was in a greasy ponytail, which looked like it had never been washed. I don't like ponytails on guys. I wonder who stumbled onto that hair style. Ya know it's sad, but I think the ponytail has ruined the appearance of a lot of clean lookin' young men. There are a lot of God's children that wear a ponytail, and I am sure He loves them, too, and probably in many cases more than some of us who don't. But, what in the heck compels them to look like that? This world seems so twisted. Girls, much to my dismay, are trying to look and act like guys; and guys, in a lot of ways, are starting — as is the case here — to look like girls. But, hey, "it's the 80s," as people say to justify their position. What can a guy like me do about it? *I just hope we as a society don't screw up this world much more than it already is, but I'm afraid we're definitely off to a good start.* I didn't make myself feel any better.

I have heard people say the ponytail acts as a filter. It keeps the people away who can't get past the ponytail, and lets those in who are not so concerned about someone's appearance. A friend told me once he knew a guy who had a real long ponytail, and the reason for it was so when he got in trouble — when he found his head in the dragon's mouth, so to speak — someone could grab him by the ponytail and pull him to safety.

After roaming this earth for about 30 years now and observing as much as possible, it is my opinion how people dress and look is pretty much commensurate to how they feel about themselves. I am not sure, but it has always appeared to me those who choose to wear a ponytail seem to be in some kind of rebellion. I sure hope my sons never do that.

As we passed the hitchhiker, I noticed he was sporting a marginally-cultivated beard, like the hippies in Missoula wore when I was in high school. I liked the look of these beards, and felt they really looked nice with those wire-rimmed glasses, like a lot of stars wore.

I suddenly found my mind on another tangent. *I wonder why so many rock stars started wearing their hair long like that?* Maybe they were all sitting around a campfire one evening, sharing a "cultural experience" with each other while puffing on one of those expensive cigarettes you can't find at the gas station, and decided to have a contest to see who could look the most ridiculous.

Everyone has to have some rational basis for anything they do; albeit good or bad. I think the reason is because no matter what we do, someone is going to disagree with us, so it's handy to have a list of excuses saved up for any occasion. Now that some people have come up with this bizarre appearance, and where society has seemed to be complacent, this is what we get.

Snapping back to the hitchhiker, I noticed he had a jacket tied around his waist, and a backpack with random items poking out, which reminds me of when I was going to college. On our campus, we were abundantly blessed with students we rednecks referred to as "granolas." I will explain this interesting species. He (as I do not remember any women falling into this category back then) would wear a curly hairdo, which was referred to — in those more conservative times — as an "afro." In order to keep his hair from getting dirty, and at the same time maintaining its style, a red or blue bandana would adorn his head. He had wire-rimmed glasses which seemed, from his standpoint at least, to be cool. He often wore a worn-out sweatshirt with the sleeves cut out near the arm pit, so any passersby could view the hair under his arms. He wore some old, reasonably-fitted cutoffs or shorts, and on his feet was a pair of what we referred to back then as "waffle stomper" shoes. They were called this because as a person walked, the shoes would leave an imprint of a waffle in the mud. This would have made for easy trackin', should they get lost and need to be rescued. These shoes would allow the granolas to safely wander into the high country where they could "find themselves" without hurting their tender feet.

I have always wondered what that meant, to *find* yourself. It reminds me of a time when I was in high school and we watched a film on the "birds and the bees." I guess the school board felt that if we students viewed this film, the likelihood of us having premarital sex may be somewhat reduced. In the film, there was a couple in this maroon and white Buick heading into a secluded area. Much to the surprise of the entire student body, the model of the car and paint job matched perfectly one owned by a fellow student. Someone immediately yelled out the name of that student. "Buster!" To the best of my recollection, the school superintendent immediately shut the projector off, and (among other things), informed us we needed to "find ourselves," all the while raucous laughter could be heard throughout the halls of the school.

The ironic thing about these tender-footed granolas, they had never even seen the high country until coming out west to go to school, but they wanted everyone to think they had grown up there. I suppose it fit well with their persona of being "one with nature," whatever that meant.

Inside their tightly-laced boots was a pair of wool socks, which they would stretch clear up to their knees with either green or red stripes near the top. Their getup, with those socks, achieved the ultimate in Eastern Idaho masculinity within the group of which they were members. To be able to maintain their social graces and intimate interaction (either with each other or nature), their backpacks contained at least a bottle of wine and a book of philosophy.

Upon a gathering of two or more of them in the same place, they would be having some heavy discussions, using words that one would never hear anywhere but in the college classroom. It seemed so out of context to hear them using these words. For lack of a better analogy, to me it was like putting a supercharger on a garden tractor. But, I did find it interesting.

It was with ardent cynicism when I would think to myself, *boy, I'm thankful I was too busy draggin' main, feedin' chickens, changin' those ignorant sprinklers pipes, or whatever it was that kept me from becoming one of those granolas.* It was obvious to me one of us was out of touch with reality here. If it was me, that was just too bad; I was still thankful.

Glancing once more at the hitchhiker, he looked to me as though had he attended college, he probably majored in Sociology or some such curriculum. It seems to me some people only use one side of their brain, which doesn't always include the part that addresses ones appearance. I think with some degrees, it's like getting a kiss from your best friend's older sister; it might feel good, but it doesn't mean much.

Isn't it ironic some of these people have spent a lot of time sucking off of the system, utilizing federal grants, getting a college education, but then they go right out into society and start fighting a lot of things the government wants to do?

I almost started sharing my next thought with my son, but decided he was far too young to understand or care. So, I kept it to myself. *If a person only plays one key on a piano, it can sound pretty bad; but, if he starts to play all the keys in some organized form, he might get what musicians refer to as a tune. With some practice, it can actually be beautiful. Therefore, one should play all the keys of the piano to have a well-balanced life.*

Well, a person can get to feeling pretty low when considering that — like the hitchhiker in my rearview mirror — no matter how bad a person appears, he has a mother like the rest of us. Can you imagine what she must go through having a son in the state of such disarray, mentally and physically? I don't imagine the majority of mothers raise their children that way, or at least we can hope. I wonder, if a young man who is not able to fit into society, perhaps has lost his job, if he ever had one, what his mother would do to help him through the rough parts of life?

I guess losing one's job can be as devastating, physically, as it was mentally for me. This sobering thought brought me back to my wife, Joyce; she has been a real trooper in trying to get me to understand how my cynical attitude is affecting me more than anyone. God love her — if her patience is stronger than my cynicism, she might just get me to change. Maybe.

64

CHAPTER 5
THE COACH

"My mom always taught me we put our pants on the same way as anyone else."

Reflecting once more on the thumbing pedestrian, I don't think there is a more humiliating experience than when one loses a job. For me, I liked my job. I felt I was accomplishing something, and was making good money from it. It is, however, rather refreshing when I look back and realize how much I have grown because of this experience. It is pretty apparent to me that God Himself had a hand in what is taking place today. The reason I believe this is how my life was going when the bottom fell out.

Though it shouldn't be this way, losing one's job can have a profound effect on a person's identity. Interestingly enough, our society has trained us to believe what we do in life is who we are. This conditioning can easily place a lid on an individual, causing him to restrict how far he may believe he can progress. I've often thought if I were to make $20,000 working in some sort of maintenance position, I believe I would have a much different opinion of myself than if I was the president of an international corporation, worth billions. Society actually separates us. The tendency is the person working a maintenance job may not consider himself "worthy" to even be in the presence of a billionaire, much less consider himself to have similar value as a human being. Proverbs 19:4 clearly makes the point: *The rich hath many friends, but the poor is separated from his neighbor.*

I have concluded that in this world, success is measured by the value of homes, vehicles, position, and most of all, money. It seldom has anything to do with character, interests, or respect. It has been my observation those who are rich have more "friends" to laugh at their jokes than those who are not. Ever notice how neighborhoods appear to be broken into classes, so lower-income housing cannot impact the property value of the rich?

My mom always taught me we put our pants on the same way as anyone else.

It is sad that people have been separated so, and I wonder if it is some kind of control measure. I don't believe it is accidental that people have been gently coerced into not associating with each other. I may be wrong, but people seem more easily controlled if they are not unified.

Anyway, it seemed I had everything going for me. My wife and I loved our four children; I had what I thought was a secure job with a local government agency; we went out to dinner at least every weekend and usually to the show; my best friend, other than my wife, lived about 200 yards down the street, which was very convenient; I was making $18,000 per year while living in a $225 a month house (which I consideer to be economic stability); I was getting heavily into golf — which I noticed improved my social status. A man I met had a P51 Mustang airplane, and he wanted me to help him with it. I wasn't an airplane mechanic, nor did I know anything about it. I believe he invited me simply because I had showed an interest, and we became friends..

In my humble opinion, I had become one of the cool people. You see, I used to wear heavy glasses in my youth and as a result, took a lot of teasing from other kids in high school. Of course my football, track, and basketball coaches had to get into the act to get laughs as well. I remember my football coach saying, "Haley, you would screw up a ship wreck." I was a pretty good athlete so I felt he was only teasing. I laughed along, but he could be very degrading to a lot of students.

I often thought about what I would find if I could peek into the brain of that coach — or any coach, actually. For some of the coaches I have become acquainted with, I don't think it would be a very time-consuming task. Most of them had class and commanded respect; however, it seemed like a couple of my coaches knew twelve, maybe thirteen vulgar phrases they apparently felt were important management tools for motivating the football team. I don't know how they functioned in society, when what they knew how to do well was only to look macho and continue to use those vulgar phrases.

When I was in junior high, I had a nasty mouth. Whenever I got mad, whatever was on my mind would come right out, unfiltered. It was pretty bad. I remember, because of my upbringing, feeling very guilty for taking the Lord's name in vain. What I did in order to conquer that problem was to substitute the 'F' word for the Lord's name. It seems for a lot of people, using the Lord's name to curse is not a big deal. In fact, for some the only "religious" experience they have is when they take the Lord's name in vain. It seems to go good with dirty jokes, in bars, sports, or whenever and wherever there is a fragile mind trying to express itself in a forceful manner. It makes sense to me where it says in the Bible, *"Thou shalt not take the name of the Lord thy God in vain,"* He actually means it. I also suspect there is a punishment for those who disregard the instruction.

Later on, I was able to pretty much conquer my weakness for using the 'F' word, as well. I suppose I'm not much better than my football coach; we all have weaknesses to overcome. I know it's wrong to stereotype all coaches, but some pretty much fit this groove.

I remember my high school football coach when I was a junior. He would always saunter down the hall like he was lookin' for a fight. To me, he looked like a 12-year-old in a 35-year-old body, chewing that gum like he was the neatest thing since flush toilets. He was a big guy, however, and could probably be successful with whomever he fought. We respected him out of fear alone, not because of his expanded mind or because he was overloaded with wisdom. It wouldn't have been such a big deal, except these individuals were supposed to be professionals. He never really impressed me with his level of intelligence.

I feel like sometimes I should be bitter about the way I was treated back then, but in retrospect it was actually a blessing. Someone once said, *"There needs to be opposition in all things."* He or she was right. A person just has to have opposition to grow. When I think about a weightlifter who wants to compete, he can't be successful if there is no resistance when he pumps iron. Humorist Josh Billings said, *"Life is like a grindstone; whether it polishes you up or grinds you into powder, depends on what you are made of."* I don't know how polished I am, but I've been ground on — a lot.

What I had going for me — and no one could take away — was the fact during my junior and senior years, I was the fastest man on both the football and track teams. This garnered a lot of respect from those who wanted to get their names in the paper and who wanted to be the best like I was, for that small window of time in my life. This helped me to maintain whatever level of self-respect I had. One day at track practice with both coaches timing me, I ran the 100 yard dash in 10 seconds flat, which not only surprised me, but flabbergasted my coaches as well. I felt pretty awesome — in some circles at least.

Because of my experience with glasses, I felt very self-conscious and it was hard to look anyone in the eye. I was told years later I was popular in school; however, because of my glasses, the girls at our school didn't want to date me. Once I started wearing contacts, my confidence bolstered.

As I reflect back, being teased changed me in many ways. I have compassion for others who face hardships. I have acquired something that most people take for granted. I spent so much time trying to make up for what I perceived as downfalls that I tried to buy and force my friendships. I no longer find it essential to try winning others' friendship. Those experiences at such an impressionable stage in my life, though insignificant then, would impact my future.

CHAPTER 6
THE HOUSE

74

"They called it dinner back then."

Driving this truck on what seems to be an endless high-way reminds me of when I used to drive a tractor to till the land. This seemed to be a never-ending chore. I would start a 20-acre field with about an eight-foot wide til-ler on the back. I learned — as I would continue to learn this more in life — I need to enjoy the journey instead of just the destination. I would put my elbow on the fender of the tractor and rest my head on my hand. I could hear the vibration of the engine and all of the operating equipment. With this noise in the background, I could think of a song and it was like the trac-tor was actually singing for me. I would spend hours listening and thinking about things as the tractor moved along the field.

"Dad," Brad questioned, pointing, "what is that thing with the long post on it?"

"I think that's called a Jackson fork, Son."

"What is it used for?" He continued staring as we drove past the machinery.

"I think it was used a long time ago for stacking hay."

"Did you ever use one, Dad?" he asked, now turning to look at me.

"No."

We saw a lot of machinery parked out in fields just waiting to rust away and be hauled off to the junk pile, and nobody seems to care. People spent their whole lives working this equipment, and it is just left here, in a forgotten metal graveyard.

"Look, Brad!" I said, with some unusual excitement. "There's a John Deere tractor, just like the one I used to drive."

Brad could not perceive the excitement I was feeling when I saw this magnificent tractor. It was one of those that had the exposed flywheel on the side. In the earlier models, the flywheel was used to start the tractor by hand. I remember mowing hay with one of those; I could drive it standing up or sitting down. The clutch consisted of a large steel lever with a ball on top to hold onto, mounted on the right side. This tractor only had two cylinders and made a cool noise. It appears nobody cares about this particular tractor — it has been abandoned and left where it was last parked. I noticed out in the field sat a large John Deere tractor, with four large tires and a cab. *Everything is new,* I thought. *The old stuff is being replaced.* Hank had a John Deere that he used to pull his hay wagon. I smiled.

There, near the John Deere, sits a hay baler; a McCormick. It is sitting there with weeds all grown up through it. *What a sad deal,* I thought. This one looks worthless, but I had a lot of fun driving ours, until it got plugged, of course. Then I would have to shut off the tractor, dismount, and unplug it by hand. Even though mechanical engineers are good, a thick stand of hay can plug a baler.

I miss baling hay, I thought to myself. Even though the tractors I drove had no cabs to keep the dust off or a stereo to listen to, I still loved driving them just the same.

I spot an old pile of sprinkler pipes, just like the ones I used to change. These have been replaced by large, circular pivots. Seems like everything has been replaced with something large, more economical, and more state-of- the-art. It makes me sad that in so many ways, the things from a simpler way of life have been shoved aside.

Just then, an old Farmall H tractor caught my eye. *It's just like the one we had,* I noted. Like the other equipment, this was sitting in a clump of weeds. One of the tires had pretty much withered away, exposing a rusted, red rim. I remember using the Farmall to pull the hay wagon. When I was younger and too little for the heavy work, I would drive the tractor while the bigger guys would buck the hay bales onto the wagon. I can still remember what it sounded like and how to start it.

I notice the old chicken coop there, has started to deteriorate to the point that it would most likely be dismantled and sold off for barn wood, which will be used in some fancy house; hope-fully, it will be as appreciated by those who purchase it now as those who purchased it back in the day.

I could hear my thoughts becoming cynical. *People sure don't keep up their houses very well. Look at that house; there are a lot of farm-ers who don't have much pride in how they look or what people think of them.* I remind myself how disappointed Joyce would be in my criticism of people I don't even know.

The house finally disappeared behind us, leaving me to pon-der the history of these farms. *No,* I thought, *I have never used a Jackson fork.* It seemed pretty archaic. What we used was a conveyor to stack bales of hay. It was powered by a gasoline engine. To use it would require someone to lean it up against the haystack, turn on the engine, and put a bale of hay on the bottom. It would then move the bale up the metal frame until it reached the top. It was fun to hurry and put as many bales on the conveyor as possible, to see if you could overwhelm the stacker on top who had to take them off one-by-one and place them. It could be a little dangerous, so we had to be careful. The conveyor has been replaced with modern equipment that will stack the hay automatically, not affording the balers the enjoyment of competing the way we had.

The Jackson fork looks like a lot of work, and I have no doubt those farmers worked really hard all of their lives. As a youngster, it never seemed to me they enjoyed life very much. They would get up in the morning around 5:00am and work in the fields 'til dark, then come in from the fields and do the other chores. I never wanted any part of it, so I left and never looked back.

The next farmhouse (as we called it) we pass is run-down, the paint is peeling off, and the grass and small trees have taken over the yard. It appears the exposed wood has deteriorated to the extent that it cannot feasibly be restored.

Looks like nobody lives here anymore, I thought. I suppose the farmers are dead now, or possibly in a nursing home, "keepin' the flies off and waiting for the end." What a payback for all of their hard work. I was guessing their kids have probably taken over the farm and have all of this new equipment to use. Again, Joyce's frustration creeps into my thoughts.

To appease my wife's consternation in my head, I re-think the notion that farmers weren't very happy; I would say they were happier then, than people are now. I doubt I have internalized this concept, but I have been taught my whole life that happiness comes from within. A farmer having a noon meal would confirm that. When noontime came, the wives would always cook a big meal for everyone, including the hired hands, and they would all come in and have dinner together. Yes, dinner. It was breakfast, dinner, and supper; nowadays we use the terms breakfast, lunch, and dinner. Can't say I know the history on how that came about.

No matter how dirty the farmers were, they would enter the house, partially dust their clothes off and wipe their feet, and the wives didn't seem to care. It was just another chore to tend to after the dishes were done.

A blessing was usually said in most households. It would be unfair to say not many continue this tradition, but with so many who snag some fast food or a TV dinner, choke it down and hardly talk to each other, I'm guessing it's not as popular as in the past. After the blessing, a great meal was enjoyed by all. Everyone laughed and enjoyed each other's company. The capstone of the meal was a large apple pie with ice cream. We didn't worry then about fat content like we do now, mostly because everything we ate was worked off in the fields.

In those days, people took care of each other. If a farmer had a problem with a piece of equipment, he could borrow his neighbor's or the neighbor would come and finish the work for him. If someone was constructing a building, others would come and help. More often than not, families would get together, do the work, and then everyone would enjoy a good barbeque. If someone had a tragedy in their family, the farmers would get together and help the family, take meals in, and all kinds of things that have become lesser seen.

The farmers' wives would hang their clothes out on a clothesline after washing. I guess it made them whiter and fresher, as opposed to throwing them in a dryer. The appliances we take for granted today were a luxury to so many families back then. I have to admit, though, I miss the smell of freshly-washed sheets that have been dried by the wind and sunshine.

Dairy farmers usually milked a large number of cows. The milk would be set out in 10 gallon cans for the milkman in a milk truck to pick up. Some of the milk was taken in and run through a separator, which was usually hand-cranked; this process would separate the cream from the milk. I wonder how many people today know exactly how the milk in that carton sitting in the store has been processed.

A lot of houses, like the old farmhouse a few miles back, had a wood stove for heat and for cooking, but likely also had electricity. The electricity, for the most part, was used for the lights. To hear the farmers talk back then, light bulbs were quite the thing. And they hardly ever went to a service station, because their gasoline supply was delivered to the farm and stored in a large gas tank.

As I think back and try to compare what it was like then to what things are like now, life really was pretty good. People were friendlier; there was less crime; money went a lot further and there weren't so many social programs as there are now. There weren't credit cards. Drug use was something you heard about, but really never noticed; people weren't worried about free healthcare; government didn't seem to bother people; folks never locked their doors; you still had silver dollars to spend; you could fix your own car. Friends didn't care what your furniture looked like; doctors would actually come to your house; you never saw or heard of graffiti being put on public and private property. People didn't wear cutoffs or pajamas when they went shopping; when you went to town, you dressed up, unless you were working. We weren't aware of any gangs in the neighborhood; when people promised you something, you could count on it; a four-wheel drive was something you used as a work truck rather than a toy. Eggs came in a bucket from the chicken coop, not from the store in cartons.

As I reviewed the list in my head, I realized I was guilty of expressing my animosity toward those in my upbringing who lived

the "simple" life — all those things I have come to prefer. Those farmers, those families who did nothing but aid their neighbors, and provided support for me, were the recipients of my limited vision on what really matters in life. As I gave some hard introspection into my attitude, I felt a knot in my gut starting to form. This time, I knew it wasn't my wife's frustration; this time — it was all mine.

82

CHAPTER 7
THE
TRUCK STOP

84

"Okay, dear, comin' right up."

"D ad?"

"What?"

Brad startled me. I was stuck deeply in my thoughts.

"What's that place?" he asked, pointing to a building that served as a gas station and convenience store.

"That's a truck stop," I answered. I knew that wasn't the end of it.

"What's it for, Dad?"

"It's so those big trucks can fill up with gas, and the truckers can eat." I saw the smile as it took over his face.

"Let's stop here and get something to drink," Brad said.

"I'm not thirsty." That was not true.

"Come on, Dad," Brad nearly whined.

Can you imagine *not* being thirsty in this part of the country? It kinda looks like there should be pyramids out here somewhere. This place probably couldn't support a small herd of camels. There's gotta be sand dunes around here some place, but I sure don't see any.

"Let's go in now, I am really thirsty," Brad begged, stretching his words to indicate his level of dehydration.

"How about we wait just one more hour?" I coaxed.

"No, Dad, I really want something to drink right now…please?"

"Okay, you convinced me."

I flipped on the blinker of that single-axle U-Haul truck and started to pull off of the interstate. The truck tried to sway as we pulled off. *We might have stacked the stuff a little too high,* I thought to myself as I over-steered a little to correct the sway. We pulled off the interchange and into the yard of the truck stop.

"Dad, look at all those trucks. Aren't they cool?" Brad's eyes opened wide; he was smitten.

"Yes," I responded, less than excited.

I remembered that, according to the U-Haul renter where we picked the truck up, we had plenty of gas to make the trip. I decided to park away from the gas pumps, where I wouldn't be in the way of the big trucks; the place was buzzing.

"Well, I guess we're here." I sat for a moment before unbuckling my seatbelt.

"Let's go in, Dad," Brad directed, unable to hide his excitement for this new adventure.

"Okay, Son." I resigned myself to obey his instruction, though

86

I sat for a moment longer.

I looked out across the parking lot. I could see the oversized fuel bays that would accommodate the tractor trailer rigs, and the typical neon beer sign in the window. My attention was drawn to a man with two young boys standing near his car. He was telling them to run over to a small tank on the edge of the property, and return. I'm guessing he was doing this to tire them out. I could relate. Not every traveling experience with restless children in the back seat is a good one. I remember being a pain to my parents, when I would fight with my sisters. On one occasion we were fighting in the back, and my father stopped the car, got out and started to walk. We hushed up fast and wondered if we'd gone just a bit too far.

The sound of a "Jake Brake" entered my ear and immediately caused my head to turn. Jake Brake was a nickname for the Jacobs Vehicle System, which was a compression braking mechanism. Nowadays the term is used for any compression brake system. They make a very loud, distinctive noise when implemented, and are unpopular with the city folk who would rather not be subjected to this particular sound. Behind the slowing tractor was a lowboy trailer with a D9 Caterpillar tractor sitting on it. *What a massive machine,* I told myself. I remember how excited I was when I was given a large Caterpillar model for Christmas as a boy.

For a fleeting moment, I thought I was a big trucker. *Sittin' high up in this U-Haul makes ya feel pretty important, just like those truckers probably think they are,* I thought. That's ridiculous. Those guys don't have as much going for them as they think. It can't take much to be a trucker. Just look at this guy over here. Isn't he something? That big gut on him is probably going to give him a heart attack. Being confined in a cab all day with no exercise would probably make anyone fat. It's hard to imagine a woman wanting a specimen like that around the house. Bet he doesn't have any other place to go or can't find any other type of work for which he is qualified. He probably didn't even finish the 8th grade.

Besides that, have ya ever heard them talk on their CB radio? They got this trucker talk meant to fool the state troopers monitoring the interstate. Seems like even the people with pickups had to have a Citizen's Band radio. They'd have two big antennas, even on their little pickups, that were about ten feet high. I guess they had them on there to be cool when they would ask the car wash attendant if he would tie them down before the pickup goes through the wash. I stopped the rant when I heard Joyce's voice in my head telling me to stop being so judgmental — an instruction she offered me routinely.

Just then, Brad ran around to my side of the truck where I was still sitting with the door open.

"What's that big yellow thing on the truck over there, Dad?" Brad asked, inquisitively.

"That is a D9 Caterpillar." I stepped down onto the ground from the cab.

As I looked at the "Cat," the question made me recall when I was young, 12 or 13 years old, and Dad let me drive a Cat on our farm to level a ditch. It was a lot of fun until I walked one of the tracks off. It made him a little upset, but he eventually was able to have it repaired.

"What do they do with them, Dad?" Brad asked, with genuine interest.

"They use them to level ground, build freeways, or make large

88

excavations. Things like that," I said, confident in my knowledge, as I was an engineer-in-training and keenly aware of construction. I thought to myself, *some of the farmers use this kind of equipment nowadays. I wonder if Hank ever did. Eh, he probably didn't even know how to start one.* I did, though, because my dad had taught me. The older Cats had what was referred to as a "pony motor," or starter motor. It was started with a pull rope, like a lawnmower, and then a lever was pulled to engage the main engine. It would spin for a few seconds, kick out a lot of smoke, and then finally start. My dad let me do it once and I thought it was pretty cool; in fact, I thought I was pretty cool.

"I want to drive one of those when I get big like you, Dad," Brad said, with enthusiasm.

You have a lot more going for you than that, I thought. People that operate this kind of equipment are about in the same class as truck drivers. The construction workers I was familiar with I had been introduced to a few years back. They didn't seem to have much of a career going, or at least any way to progress as they basically did the same thing throughout their employment history. It was funny to watch them when I first became involved in engineering. I found them interesting, and my observation was they usually wore cowboy boots and blue jeans. Some completed the ensemble with cowboy hats, others wore baseball-styled hats with bills.

It seems that our culture has designated those who have to work hard, physically, wore hats. There is nothing negative I can identify about wearing hats on the job; in fact I think it's an important source of protection. But, they wore them everywhere, including movies, and even into church, if they could get away with it.

What bothers me about hats is a lot of people find it neces-

sary and appropriate to wear hats inside buildings, like restaurants or churches. It appears that our civility has pretty much leaked out. When I was real young, there was hardly ever anyone inside a building wearing a hat; it was customary for people to remove their hats before entering. Now it seems there is minimal regard for this eroding cultural facet. I think it would simply be a real hoot (if I were big and strong enough!) to walk up to someone in a restaurant who had forgotten to take his hat off, and while looking him in the eye take his hat off and carefully set it on the table. Then, with slow and careful speech, I would quietly inform him to leave it there until he was ready to go outside. *Wouldn't that be great?* I fantasized. *Why, he would probably start huffing and puffing, and commence to utilize all those vulgar words that seem to be hardwired into his vocabulary.* But, since I am not big and strong, I won't.

I remember once when my father-in-law and I were driving a small tractor back to his house. When we were about to pass the house of an old mechanic who always had the brim of his hat flipped up, my father-in-law flipped his up and waved to him. I really got a kick out of that ritual of camaraderie.

Heavy laborers' shirts are of different types that seem to vary with their personality, mood, or the weather. I rarely see them wear any kind of coat; my guess is a coat would conflict with their macho persona. If they didn't smoke cigarettes, in most cases, it would be easy to see the impression of a chewing tobacco can in their back pocket, about to wear clean through the denim material. I knew a construction worker who always wore a hard hat while working on the survey crew. It seemed this hat was threaded somehow so he could screw it onto his head with a wrench. He never took it off when entering a building, nor would I be surprised if it remained in place for all his daily activities. This is the way I remember it at least. I don't remember them taking it off when they are in the presence of a lady.

Speaking of ladies, it is not beneath the dignity of some con-struction workers, I observed, to swear in front of a lady and just be downright vulgar. I wasn't raised to disrespect women, and it gets my hackles up to witness such behavior. If I was a fighting man, I would put some of these men in their place. The irony is, I suppose, the women these men are being so cal-lous around appear not only unoffended, but carry their own with the profanity. So, had I challenged one of them, I would have probably spilled some blood for nothing. I guess it just goes to show you that people tend to gravitate toward their own kind.

Construction workers I've known are typically pretty tough and are a lot bigger than I, so I really have no desire to mess with them. I could easily find myself on my back at the drop of a hat. *But, as they never take their hats off, there is never a hat to drop —* I chuckle to myself. I've always figured either their self-esteem or their egos — perhaps both — are very fragile, and fighting is the only way they know how to deal with it. To protect my-self from a construction worker's wrath, I tend to make sure they know I realize their physical superiority, and that seems to subside any potential issue. It never hurts to fluff their egos occasionally.

A few years ago, I was the inspector on a job site. It was a real hot day and, as a result, the concrete was setting up faster than the contractors could finish it. I was having a conversation with one of the guys, perhaps the owner, when suddenly and with-out any warning, he started just a cussin' and throwing things. I thought even though I was the ultimate authority on the job site and I could have shut the job down because of conduct like that, I knew I had better get out of the way, and fast. After the outburst, it took me some time to get him mellowed out, but he finally settled down.

I'm not totally convinced the rest of society is aware of this, but it has been my observation the "life blood" of many construction workers is beer; not any of that "near beer," but just plain beer. There's just no other way to say it. They live for it, they use it to chase women, they fight with a can of it in one hand, and at least half of their personality makeup is a direct result of its consumption. Their weekly schedules are centered on drinking beer, and the lack of it makes their personalities function at less-than-optimum level. Advertisers incorporate construction workers into beer ads and commercials. But, ironically, I could not identify any alcoholics, or at least from what I could tell; they took care of their responsibilities and work. I have no idea what the life expectancy of a construction worker is with a lifestyle like that, but it seemed like they were handling it okay, back when I was introduced to them.

I remember trying beer. I just never took hold of the practice for at least a couple reasons: I had four friends that were killed in a drunk-driving tragedy, and my sister who was beaten by her alcoholic husband. I suppose that sort of thing has a big effect on a guy so coupled with my beliefs, experiences, and observation, I've chosen to stick with other less-glamorous beverages, like water — a decision I will never regret. It has become apparent to me that among some other things, like money, beer separates people. I have noticed as I have gotten older, it seems more beer is being consumed by society. It would be interesting to find out what the annual cost of alcohol is on our society regarding lives, property, and money lost.

This particular species of the labor force I've met like to play pool, sometimes rodeo, chase women, fight, and hangout at the bars every Friday and Saturday night. But, they were always at work on time every Monday morning and ready to give their all. I was impressed, especially when I knew the majority of these people lived on a farm of some type where they were tending to horses and cows or some other domestic animals. I suppose they could be considered a new hybrid of farmers — holding down manual labor jobs as well as what was required to manage a farm.

I thought about my internal dialogue and realized how much I had boxed-in the willing workers with stereotypes. To be honest, I don't know if stereotypes create the behaviors, or if the behaviors create the stereotypes. Either way, I was starting to take the time to think about what my wife had been trying to get me to understand.

As I looked at the Cat, I remembered what Brad had asked and I hadn't yet answered. He seemed too mesmerized by the machine to have noticed, though.

"I don't think you want to drive one of those, Son. It's hard work and will make you get old before your time." I figured that comment might detour him from considering heavy labor as future employment. I have always wanted my kids to have careers that were in the category of professionals. But, I also decided whatever they do, as long as it is legal, I will support them.

Out of the corner of my eye, I glimpsed a man I presumed to be a truck driver approaching me. He was big and wore some faded green pants held up with suspenders. I guess once a person's circumference exceeds his belt capacity, the belt is no longer functional and is replaced by suspenders.

"So, where ya headed?" he inquired, his tone friendly and his voice deep and raspy.

I was kinda caught off-guard. I hadn't heard one of them speak before. I would see them in their trucks driving, or sittin' in a café. I haven't had the occasion, other than on a C.B., to actually hear one talk. (I swear I heard Joyce groan at my description, as though truckers are a rare breed of animal recently discovered in the United States.)

"Oh, we're just headin' down I84," I replied, trying to mimic the dialect of this uncommon species; I didn't think it would take much to talk like one. I didn't want to tell him exactly where I was going so I shared very little information. My reasoning for this — a person can't really trust people anymore, and I didn't want to take any chance that he might follow us or something.

"Where are *you* headed?" I asked, directing the conversation back to him.

"I'm movin' a family over to Portland." He thumbed toward his semi behind him. "I feel sorry for them; they don't seem to have much, and what they do have ain't in good shape."

I wondered why he felt comfortable talking to me about them. He seems to be a thoughtful man.

"Don't they call the truckers that move people 'Bed Bugs' on the C.B.?" I asked with a smile, already knowing the answer.

"Yep, that's our handle, a'ight," he said, with some pride. "Do you live around here?"

"No," I replied, getting concerned about his interest. "Why do you ask?" He didn't answer my question, nor did he pry further.

"This sure is pretty country," he said, and took a sip of whatever was in his well-used travel thermos.

I thought to myself, *surely you don't believe that, especially after driving*

all over the United States. Look at this place!

"Come on, Dad, let's go in," Brad begged, yanking on my arm.

"Okay, Son," I said, a bit thankful for his insistence. "Looks like I better go in," I said to the trucker, and gave the "knowing nod" which often substituted a traditional greeting, but I also reached out to shake his hand. Surprisingly, I noticed they were rough and calloused. It made me wonder if he worked on a farm in order to make ends meet. When I looked into his eyes, a level of sincerity and humility etched in his countenance caught my attention and made we wonder, *have I misjudged this man?*

To ignore the uncomfortable query in my conscience, I quickly declared, "Okay, I guess I will see you later."

"I am sure you will," he said with a smile and that indigenous truck-driver drawl.

This is what they call a truck stop, I thought, *replaying my answer to Brad. Haven't had the occasions to drop by one of these joints for a long time. This one sure is a big place.* Brad and I walked in.

Off to the right were three pinball machines, all of which were occupied and offered a constant chiming of electronic bells. Standing at the game at the far end was another trucker-lookin' fellow, a truck-driver-stereotype personified. A large number of truckers are overweight, at least with regard to the health standards the government is currently endorsing. Another clue I use for identifying truck drivers is their wallet, which is usually connected to their belt with a chain — *a "chain driven" wallet,* I thought. I always got a chuckle out of myself with that comment, usually followed by a dry "Aren't you clever" response from my wife.

It seemed like this trucker was getting tense and pretty angry with his electronic nemesis, so I decided to watch him. He put his quarter in, gave the lever a pull to flip the ball up to start another game. He then grabbed the machine with both hands. Each time he pushed the buttons to activate the flipper he would usually hit and shake the machine. At one point, he shook the machine so hard I thought it was going to trip the tilt sensor. He was just goin' after it like a wild dog on raw meat.

Finally, the ball had taken a bad bounce and disappeared through that ugly port, announcing to him (and everyone else within earshot of the machine) that he was done. "Game Over." He then gave the machine a big smack on its side, followed up with a push, took the Lord's name in vain, and shuffled away.

I thought to myself, *why these people get so upset when they play and lose to those stupid pinball machines is beyond me.* I didn't see anywhere on the machine — and I've looked to make sure — where it says a person could win money. What do people expect? A fella would really have to be a fool to play a pinball machine with any high expectations. A player will usually lose their money; they seem annoyed because they chose to play the stupid game, spending what they can (or not) afford to lose, and are unable to win any rounds. When the game ends, the pinball machine doesn't say "thank you for your money," or "please, come back," because the folks who designed it know people will do so on their own. It's as though some of these people *like* to lose money over and over, and keep coming back for more. It's amazing how people make money by ripping each other off. What's really crazy about it is, the people getting ripped off must actually like it, or seem to, anyway.

I remember the well-known phrase: *Screw me once, shame on you. Screw me twice, shame on me.* Because of his kindness and love for others, as I grew up I watched my Dad get taken advantage of by others. So much so, I decided I would not knowingly put myself in those situations. Sadly, because of that decision, I have focused on myself more than what I could do for others. I've been more likely to say to someone in need, "Sorry about your luck; hope you can find your way out of the mess you're in," rather than lending a hand, my time, a tool, or whatever someone may have been in need of. As I thought about this, I had a twinge in my stomach, and knew it was shame. This is not how my father raised me and he would be sad if he knew how I felt.

I guess the reason I seem so pompous about those pinball games is, when I was seven or eight years old my family always attended the annual County Fair where we would go on opening day. On one particular night, I was watching someone at the carnival play with a steam shovel game that picks up toys or whatever for you from inside of a glass cage, if you are so lucky. The way they worked is, the player would deposit the money and turn a crank on the game. As the crank was turned, the shovel would hover over the prizes. The faster the crank was turned, the faster the shovel moved. When the player got the shovel over the toy he wanted, he would stop cranking; then by resuming the cranking the shovel would lower itself down onto the toy and begin to close, trying to pick up the toy. If you miss the toy, the shovel continues to go on its merry way, finishing the turn. Of course, the best toys were laid up against the glass where the shovel will never reach, or are buried in the sawdust just enough to where you can still see them, but the shovel can't pick them up.

This one particular year there was a knife I really liked and wanted. It had about an eight-inch blade as I recall, with a hand guard and a pearl handle. It was really pretty, and I wanted it. I spent no less than $5.00, as best as I can remember, trying to win that knife but the only ones who ever won, seemed to me, were the carnival workers. These people were known as "carnies," a title pinned on one who works around or is employed by a carnival. They are an interesting species with a culture all their own.

When I was a boy they were not very old; usually somewhere between 18 and 40 years of age. Many of them have longer hair than most, which seemed to have significantly more oil than the normal daily production of hair follicles. It was the exception if a carnie did not have a cigarette hanging out of his mouth together with the customary squint, which protects their eyes from smoke the Surgeon General refers to on the back of each pack of the cigarettes, claiming could be "harmful to your health." Carnies, for the most part, didn't dress all that well, either. They normally wore a dark shirt and dark pants (which seemed odd to me, as it was usually hot during carnival events), and motorcycle boots. I assumed these folks somehow got displaced after leaving school. But I am not completely sure that many of them graduated or even had the opportunity to attend school at all.

The carnies I've met didn't have the tendency of being very verbose, except when they are manning a booth where you throw darts, shoot guns or play basketball. Then, they can actually gravitate to becoming obnoxious, yelling at and coaxing at a person to "play the game and win a prize." I have learned, because of my experience with the knife, I can walk away from any deal, all the way from a car to a pen knife, whether associated with a carnie or not.

I recall on a recent occasion being indirectly affected by this culture. I was waiting for my son to get off of one of those rides that turns the rider upside-down. After exiting the ride, he told me he had lost his wallet. We looked around for a moment, then someone informed us the attending carnie had grabbed it. We asked the carnie about it, but with shrugged shoulders and a blank stare, he failed to produce the item. We finally scrounged up the Sheriff, who — with much intimidation, finger-pointing and debate — was able to get my son's wallet returned.

Anyway, that knife I just *had* to have made me feel rotten. I remember feeling badly because I knew my parents couldn't afford to spend that kind of money on a crummy toy. I will never forget what I learned from that experience, and I now marvel at the money I save because I learned the value of a dollar.

"Dad, can I play this machine?" Brad asked, his eyes fixated on the lights of the game.

"Probably." I reached in my pocket and pulled out a couple of dimes. *That's not going to be enough to play the game*, I thought with some disgust. *I really don't want Brad to waste any money on such foolishness.* "I'll have to go get some change. Be right back," I muttered, and headed for the front counter.

I hesitated for a moment and realized Brad probably shouldn't be left alone in a place like this. You never know what these odd, social outcasts might do, especially those from the big city. You hear all kinds of stories about truck drivers who are nuts and do awful things to people. I motioned to him to come by me, where I was standing near the cash register.

"I need some change for the pinball machine," I asked, shyly.

Standing on the other side of the cash register was a lady. She had a warm smile and was friendly to me. She had curly brownish red hair, with some of that maroon lipstick and eye shadow. She was older, but she dressed very young. *Maybe she feels like she has to compete with the younger women*, I surmised. There on the other side of the cash register, I noticed a smoking cigarette in the ashtray. *Why?* I asked myself. *Why do people have to smoke?* I remember there were girls in our school that smoked. I thought it was degrading to them. When people smoke, they almost always have a squinted look on their faces. I think smoking really ages a person.

When I was younger, I remember finding some cigarette butts near a haystack on our farm. My brother and I put one in our mouths, and thought it was pretty cool. Sometime later, we had a butt and had gotten some matches. We tried smoking them, but they weren't as cool as we made them out to be.

"Here's your change, honey," the clerk said, placing the coins into my hand, her words dripping with intentional charm. It was very hard not to notice the long, red claws she was sporting on the ends of her fingers.

"Thank you," I said, and directed Brad over to an unoccupied pinball machine. I gave Brad a quarter and showed him where to place it in the machine. As he released a pinball, which started the game, I looked up at the main display of the machine and noticed a picture of a nearly-naked lady. *Why do they have to have this kind of stuff around where the kids can see it?* It seems like the world tries every subtle way it can to pollute the minds of the youth.

"Dad," Brad blurted out, "I almost have 50 points."

"That's good," I responded, not expressing any excitement.

"As soon as I get a hundred, I will win a game!" His enthusiasm was so endearing. *I sure hope he doesn't get hooked on a stupid pinball machine like my roommate in college did,* I thought. As the bells continued chiming for Brad, my thoughts wandered back in time.

If my roommate, Denny, couldn't find someone else addicted to pinball like he was to hang out at the arcade, he would always beg me to go with him. He would get his money out of his drawer and, with lots of excitement and enthusiasm on his part, we would head off down the sidewalk. When we would get to the arcade, he

100

would scope out the games and attack. "Look here. Someone has left some games on this machine," he would whisper to himself in a predatory tone.

I swear Denny would almost overdose on the adrenaline rushing through his veins. He'd get so excited that, when he tried to get the money out of his pocket, it would flip out all over the floor. I was expected to pick up the scattered coins, so as not to disrupt his pinball "high." After picking up the money, I would just keep it in my hand, knowing he would need it soon.

As I would watch him play, I would always wonder why a college kid, who is supposed to be more mature and intelligent after graduating high school, would allow himself to get hooked on a pinball machine. I have to admit, though, he was really good at it. Sometimes he would have to leave games on the machine and walk away. I'm sure I saw tears forming in the corners of his eyes. I remember on more than one occasion when he would try to sell the games to a less-skilled pinball wizard at a cheaper rate. When I witnessed these transactions I always thought to myself, *this is crazy*.

While Denny was salivating over his mechanical rival, I would lean on it and every so often, when I thought he wasn't paying attention, I would bump the machine just hard enough to trip the tilt sensor. When the sensor was tripped, he would slowly turn to me in a weird way that would make me laugh, and would commence to issue a threat, followed by this big lecture about how I "needed to grow up and learn to respect what other people were trying to do." If I caused him to lose his quarter before the game was finished, I would graciously consent to give him one of mine. I didn't like doing it; but tripping the game was the only buzz I would get while being around those inane machines.

"Dad, look! I just got 110 points!" Brad squealed.

This is deja vu, I thought. *How can I ever keep him from playing these stupid pinball machines?*

"Darn it," Brad finally said. "I lost my last ball. Do you have some more money, Dad?"

"No," I said with a tone of disgust.

My son's disappointment led him down another path. "Let's get something to munch on. Okay?"

We walked to the corner of the room and sat down in a booth. Whenever I go to a restaurant or cafeteria, I would rather sit in a booth. I do not like sitting at those tables out in the middle of the room. The booths are a lot more comfortable than the hard dining chairs. I also like to sit in the corner where I can see what's going on. I'd heard stories about how people who have been in a war sit against the wall so they could always see what was going on. It doesn't even matter if people are smoking next to me; I still like the booths better. It bugs me when I can't see what's going on around me, so a booth against the wall gives me the best vantage point.

"How are you guys, today?" our waitress asked with a grin.

"We're doing real well," I replied, trading smile-for-smile.

"Is this your son?" she asked, laying on the charm.

"Yes."

"He's sure a good lookin' kid, just like his dad," she said, winking.

"I guess so," I said, feeling the red overtaking my face.

"Looks like we're going to get some rain," the waitress said, sharing the same grin she had a few seconds earlier.

"Ya, looks like the scorpions out here are gettin' their..."

I could tell the server was distracted and not really listening to my words. "What did you say?" she asked politely, but her eyes were fixed on something else.

"Nothing."

I'll bet the scorpions get real thirsty before they ever get a drink. It looks like it's gotten so dry out here even the cacti have all died off. I can't believe people actually live in this part of the country. I don't even think *Hank* would live out here. Somebody told me once where they grew up wasn't the arm pit of the earth, but you could see it from there. I think it applies to this area as well.

"What would you boys like?" came the question, our server now focused on Brad and me again.

"Brad, here, wants some sausage and eggs. I'll have the hash browns and gravy," I ordered, handing her the menus.

"Okay, dear, comin' right up." She turned and walked our order to the kitchen, returning her pencil to its place behind her ear.

It's kinda flattering to be called dear, but it is also embarrassing, when my son is sittin' here listening. Ya never know what kids will say when they get a chance to talk to their moms. They really like to spill the beans if they can. I know I took great

103

pleasure in tattling when I was a young boy.

The way this waitress is acting, either she believes in love at first sight, or she is just working for a tip. I find it annoying when people suck up to others to sell something, and as soon as they get the money, they have no concern at all. *She doesn't care how we're doin'. She's just trying her best to get a tip,* I guessed in my head. It's probably really not her fault. After all, society has raised us to sell in one way or another, and I suppose she is not working here for the fun, slingin' hash; she has to make a living.

After our food was served, Brad became engrossed in a comic book offered to the under-12 patrons. It was easy to monitor when the storyline became interesting as Brad would stop chewing, then returned to shoveling his breakfast in when the plot settled down.

With Brad content, my thoughts wander to human behavior. There are a lot of things about life that are phony. It seems to me when we are young, we see all the glitter and grandeur. We aren't aware of what's on the other side of the facade people present; often there is an unpainted, rough-cut surface hidden beneath the layers of perceived magnificence. As we grow older, for some, we notice the back of the prop as much or even more than the front where all the glitter is.

I recall visiting an old church that served as a tourist attraction. I don't remember having to pay, but we were allowed in to see it. There were no pews; only a wooden floor. In addition to some crosses, on the walls hung some other religious artifacts and paintings of Native Americans attending services. Near the front of what I would call the chapel stood a very old podium, covered on three sides by a decorated, plaster surface. However, the back side of the pulpit where the preacher would stand was uncovered, leaving the gray, exposed wood framing to deteriorate. Interesting to me was the fact the three sides were obviously decorated for show,

and since the back side could not be seen by the congregation, it was left in a shabby state.

I remember when Joyce and I were first married, we were called upon by an insurance salesman. I guess in order for the insurance companies to keep up with their competitors, an agent would read the legal section to see what new marriage licenses had been granted during the previous week. After compiling an extensive list, he would head out of his office looking for some new customers. When this particular agent arrived at our house, he was overly-friendly, which included looking at pictures of our family and saying how wonderful they looked. Then, he proceeded to tell us how important it was that we be insured. If that wasn't enough, he presented multiple policies and explained them to us, including a rehearsed dissertation of how devastating it could be if we didn't purchase some life insurance. He spoke to us as though we understood what he was talking about. I really don't think he expected this young, gullible couple to say we weren't interested; he continued the pressure to purchase his insurance until it was crystal clear he was no longer welcome. After that, if we happened to see him on the street, he wouldn't speak. His sales pitch had been all show. No more, no less.

CHAPTER 8
THE CHOPPER

"I soon realized that, in a small way, I was one of them."

"**L**ook at that motorcycle!" Brad blurted out with excitement. I looked out the window next to where we were sitting for breakfast, and spotted the motorcycle that had just pulled into the lot.

"How would you like to ride that, Son?" I asked, nudging him lightly.

"It would be fun, Dad. Let's get a small motorcycle so I can ride it. Okay, Dad?" Brad asked, his eyes gleaming.

Ya, that would be great, I thought to myself, but just smiled in response.

The bike was sittin' against the curb in the parking lot next to us so it was easy to see. It was in mint condition, flawless and shiny. It was a Harley, alright. I knew my motorcycles. I admired the deep blue, metal flake paint, with everything else in chrome but the tires. It had been rebuilt and converted into what I knew to be called a "chopper".

It was obvious to me this extraordinary bike wasn't owned by a farmer or business man. The guy sittin' on it didn't seem to belong to either of those tribes. *He must be a hippie or one of those savage bikers ya hear about all the time.* He was wearing some kind of dirty black vest-looking thing, which appeared to be a leather shirt with the sleeves torn off. Poking out of the sleeve on my side was an oversized arm, with a very large tattoo of a dragon or something. It would appear riding the bike finally caused his stomach to blow the bottom button out of the vest, leaving his gut to hang out underneath. His hair was done up nicely in a ponytail which hung about half way down his back. His boots were mostly worn-out and covered with grease.

He had on a pair of those small sunglasses, a dark blue, with each lens about an inch-and-a-half in size. *Pretty functional for a motorcycle,* the sarcasm dripping in my thoughts. *They aren't safety glasses, that's for sure. I wonder how they would hold up if a bumblebee hit them at 70 or 80 miles an hour. I'll bet after an event like that he would be looking for another pair of glasses.*

I wonder if research is done on sunglasses. Maybe experiments that, while a guy is wearing a pair like the motorcycle rider is sporting, a couple of lab technicians would fire frozen bumblebees at his glasses, using some sophisticated, high-powered air gun. This would be similar to when researchers freeze chickens and fire them at airplane windshields. To determine the ultimate safety of the glasses, the bees could be fired with a velocity in excess of the highest, anticipated speed at which cyclists would travel; in this case, probably pretty fast. After each shot, some field data would be collected from which they would measure, post-impact: elevation of his temper, eye damage, and damage to the glasses.

He must get something out of wearing them. *How can he look that way?* I countered. *At what point in his life did he decide this costume was vogue?* Maybe he was raised this way. His father might have liked Harleys, just as it appears he does.

Just then, his wife or girlfriend walked up and got on the back of the bike. They look alike, actually, with similar profiles as they sat

on the bike together. Almost looks like one of those paintings ya might find in an old magazine for cigarette advertisements. I suppose the law of attraction is at work; everyone gravitates to someone like them. *He looks like a mean son-of-a-gun,* I thought to myself. *I wonder what he would do if I went out there and said something bad about his bike.* I reminded myself I have always been afraid to fight because I don't like gettin' hurt. I don't remember watching very many fights where even the "winner" walked away without shedding some blood.

Staring at this Harley reminds me of when I was about twelve years old and we had a hired man to help with bringing in the hay. He had a Harley. It wasn't as nice as this one, but it was big and fast. Every day after he got off work, he would take my brother and me for a ride. I remember how important I felt looking down and watching the shadow of the bike as we moved along the road. I thought how cool Harleys were because the gear shift was up by the gas tank, and you shifted it by hand like you would a truck.

Just then our bikers slowly moved away.

"Are you finished eating?" I asked Brad.

"Yes. Let's go out and see if the motorcycle is still out there!" he said, standing up quickly.

"I think it's gone now, Son."

I saw the disappointment build up in Brad's face and I felt bad for him. I remembered how much I wanted to be around motorcycles when I was his age.

"Are ya ready to go?" I asked with some enthusiasm, trying to lift his spirits a little.

"Ya. I guess," was the reply, his tone indicating I wasn't successful.

We paid for the meal and walked outside. There, parked away from the gas pumps, was the chopper we had been looking at. I looked around to see where the owner was. I always like to assess the situation, so I know what is going on.

"Look, Dad," Brad yelled with excitement, "there's the motorcycle. Come on, Dad, let's go look at it. Okay?"

What could I say? "I guess."

I was admittedly a little nervous about going over by the bike because the owners weren't anywhere to be found. I certainly didn't want to anger *those* bike owners. We strolled over by the bike, and I became interested as Brad's excitement took some of my nervousness away.

"Dad, why does the wheel stick out so far and why do the handle-bars stick up that way?" Brad asked, pointing to everything he saw. I made him shove his hands in his pants pockets to avoid touching the motorcycle. I made myself do the same.

"Other than to really be cool, I don't know," was my response. I don't remember hearing or reading if there was any practical reason for the extended front forks, but I continued my answer. "I suppose so the driver can sit back in the seat and still be able to reach 'em." Sounded kinda ridiculous, but it was the only thing I could think of.

Brad immediately reached up, grabbed the throttle, and started twisting it. I was mortified.

"Don't do that, Son! Remember how mean-looking those people

were when they were sitting on the bike? They might..."

"Hey, boy! What ya doin' there?" came a voice from behind me.

Indescribable terror shot through my body. *You've stuck your foot in now,* I thought. It seemed all of the blood had completely vacated my head. My legs were weak and I wanted to sit down. I fought to regain my composure so that, hopefully, the man wouldn't focus on what I had just said or how scared I was.

"You like choppers?" he asked Brad.

Brad and I had both stepped back a little. Apparently he hadn't heard what I said. Upon discovering this, I started to relax a little. Ya always hear how mean these people are, so I didn't know what to expect. *I really don't want to be around this guy, but it might be a little uncomfortable to leave right now,* I thought.

"Yes," Brad responded, with a shy grin.

"Do ya wanna sit on 'er?" the man asked my son.

Brad looked at me with wide eyes, obviously not picking up on my internal terror.

"Go ahead, Son," I said, with a forced smile.

I'm not yet sure what to think of this guy. He seems to be friendly, but ya never can be too sure. I walked over by Brad on the bike. *I might be able to protect him if something happens,* I thought. After all, this guy is really over weight, looks like he has been smokin' for the better portion of his life, and I don't see a knife or gun on him. *He is big as a house, though.*

113

He took off his sunglasses and reached his hand out to me. Both actions caught me a little off-guard. "My name is Mike; my friends call me Hawk," he professionally asserted.

I reluctantly grabbed his hand. "My name is Gary, Gary Haley," I clumsily responded.

"Gary, it's nice to meet you. I guess this is your son?"

I nodded. "Ya, this is Brad."

"So, what grade are you in, Brad?"

I couldn't believe how professional-sounding this guy was. *How could he be so articulate, have a nice bike and then look like he does?*

"I'm in the second grade," Brad said with pride.

"Gary, I want you to meet my wife. Honey, come over here and meet these fine people."

Why does he think we are fine? He doesn't even know us.

His wife was standing near the pop machine, which was next to the store. She seemed to be caught up in her own conversation with someone. *This guy is, in spite of how he looks.* His wife walked over to where we were standing.

"Honey, I want you to meet Gary and Brad Haley. This is my wife, Vonda." His eyes held a genuine fondness for this woman.

"Hi, Vonda. It's nice to meet you," I stated, accepting her out-reached hand as well. I didn't know if I really meant what I said, so I felt a little hypocritical about saying it.

114

"Where are you fellows from?" she inquired. Her interest seemed sincere.

"I was born in Idaho, but grew up in western Montana," I shared.

"Oh, what part?" I noticed her interest, again, was piqued.

"Near Corvallis."

"We knew some people from that area. In fact, Mike knew a Haley when he worked at a concrete plant in Missoula. Re-member, honey?" Mike nodded and I could tell he was trying to recall a name.

"That's interesting," I said. "What was his name?"

"Leon Haley," came his answer.

"That's my dad!" I blurted out, and immediately heard the high pitch of my voice.

"We really like him. He is a good man, but we haven't seen him for a while," Vonda said. "He was very nice to us. He helped us get our car started once when we were stranded." Her smile revealed her appreciation.

I thought to myself, *my dad was kind to a lot of people. Obviously he didn't show any prejudice toward them.*

"Well, Brad, how would you like to go for a ride?" Mike asked, bending down eye-to-eye with my son.

"Yes! Yes, please!" he exclaimed. *The high-pitched voice must be a hereditary thing,* I noted.

Oh, I don't know about this, I thought to myself, as Brad and Mike were straddling the bike. *I wonder if I can trust these people,* I considered as Mike strapped a helmet onto Brad's head. This was not something I would ordinarily allow my son to do. Vonda must have sensed my concern and said, "Gary, Brad will be alright. Mike will be careful." She seems to be a real caring and sensitive person. It's amazing she looks intimidating in her leather riding clothes, and yet is so kind and intuitive.

Mike replaced those nice sunglasses on his face. He then set the choke, twisted the throttle, stood up on the kick starter, and dropped his weight. That pretty blue chopper sputtered and started. There is no other piece of machinery on the face of God's green earth that can duplicate the sound of a Harley. It sounded great, especially after he revved it up a couple of times.

"Hold on, Brad!" Mike yelled over the loud motor. Brad braced his knees into the seat, and squeezed Mike around the waist.

About that time, he barked the tire, and the bike shot forward. *How cool,* I thought to myself. Those bikes are so amazing. I always get excited whenever I hear that Harley growling noise. Mike drove the bike to the highway, stopped, and took off down the road. With Brad hangin' on for dear life, Mike punched it and ran through all the gears. In just a few seconds, the sound faded in the distance.

I sure hope they come back. I can't believe I let Brad ride with someone like Mike, scolding myself the way I knew Joyce would if she saw what I did. I decided I would try to be polite and friendly to Vonda. Under usual circumstances, I probably wouldn't make much of an effort to speak to her.

"So, where are you from, Vonda?" I asked.

116

"I was born in Portland and moved to Missoula when I was 15."

"Why would you want to move to Missoula?" I asked, sounding much more judgmental than I intended. But, Missoula had the pulp mill there and it had a terrible smell that moved all the way down the Bitterroot Valley where I lived. I could see sadness building up in Vonda's face. I found myself becoming embarrassed for her and I wasn't even sure why.

"My dad had to go to prison," she confessed on his behalf. "They wouldn't let me live with my mom, so I had to go stay with my grandma." She seemed so wounded and I started feeling sorry for her. It kinda stunned me that she felt comfortable enough to tell me about her past. *What can I say to make her feel better?* I wondered. *I can't believe I am having this conversation. How did this happen?*

"It's ok that you lived with yer grandma. It doesn't look like it's your fault, and you don't need to worry about your past." Though I felt like I came across a little disingenuous, I really believe what I said. I believe many are strangled by their past, not necessarily because of what happened, but because they keep bringing it forward and allowing it to penalize and dam them from achieving what they want from their lives. We need to emotionally and mentally leave our past in the past. Yes, it is easier said than done, but if mastered, we would be able to move beyond the hurt, be happier and more productive. I remember this principle being taught through the analogy of plowing a field. The plowman sees an immovable object in the distance and keeps his eye on it. In that manner, the row will be straight. If, on the other hand, he continues to look back, the row will be crooked.

"I know," she said. "I just can't let it go."

Feeling incredibly awkward and wanting to change the subject I asked, "How did you meet Mike?"

"We met while we were going to college in Missoula."

"At the University?" I asked, thrilled that she was smiling again.

"Yes. Mike rescued me," Vonda answered, laughing. "He worked a couple of jobs so we could both get through school."

"What did he do?" I inquired.

"Oh…he was a trucker and a construction worker." She didn't hesitate a moment to announce her husband's careers.

Wow, I thought to myself, *a trucker and a construction worker. In spite of all that, he seems professional.* My mind drifted back to my very limited experience as a construction worker and a truck driver.

I worked for a small city in Montana. There, my duties consisted of driving a gravel truck, being an oil distributor, and working in the parks. I enjoyed hauling gravel from a stockpile to streets we were rebuilding. My boss, Jim, functioned as the Street Superintendent and Chief of Police. He always maintained a gruff exterior, but — as would be revealed to me later — was soft-hearted inside. On one occasion, while pulling into the yard where the stockpile of gravel was, I was temporarily blinded by the sun resulting in my not seeing a power pole directly in my path. Though I was moving slowly, I "center-punched" it. I immediately stopped the truck and jumped out to assess the damage. To my horror, the front bumper was noticeably bent in at the center with the ends protruding forward from their original alignment. After a few quick glances in every direction, it became apparent Jim had not witnessed the incident, bringing me momentary relief. While maintaining a moderate amount of anxiety, I slowly climbed back into the truck. *How*

will I tell him? I thought, trying to quell the knot in my stomach. I pulled the truck around near to the loader-mounted tractor where Jim was seated. After stopping the truck, my boss dismounted the tractor and walked around the front of the truck, apparently to talk to me. As I said, this man was very gruff, had a hard face, and — for someone like me — a mean countenance.

After walking around the newly-dented truck, he stopped, turned around, surveyed the bumper, and slowly looked over at me. I couldn't keep from laughing and didn't bother trying. He got a smirk on his face I was very grateful to see and I don't remember anything ever being said about that mishap again.

I remember the time when I was dumping gravel and he was on the road grader. After dumping, he motioned for me to pull up by the grader. I rolled down the window to talk. About that time, the mayor (Jim's boss) pulled up. The mayor got out and walked to the grader, and as he approached, Jim yelled out, "What the hell do you want?" At that point, with the truck door open, I nearly fell out of the truck from laughing. But, it's easy to laugh when you're not on the receiving end of that bark.

Thinking back to those construction workers and truck drivers I soon realized that, in a small way, I was one of them. I felt ashamed as my previous judgmental thoughts flooded my mind.

"So, what did you guys major in at school?" I asked, curious.

"Mike has a Bachelor's in Mechanical Engineering, and I have a degree in Political Science," she said with subtle pride.

Impressive, I thought to myself. These people are educated and present themselves well in conversation. I was becoming aware

that Vonda's manner of dress wasn't bothering me as it had at first. She seemed to be a nice person, with a personality one couldn't help but like.

I could hear the sound of the chopper as it came within earshot of us. I must have been nervous all the while they were gone because, upon hearing that noise, I felt my muscles relax.

"Now, didn't I tell you they would be alright?" Vonda asked, patting me on the shoulder.

"Yes, you did," I responded with a sheepish grin. My eyes immediately dropped down and I found myself staring at an ant that had just crawled out of a crack in the pavement. I wondered to myself, while feelings of embarrassment crept into my heart, *why have I always had such a negative attitude about people like Mike and Vonda, or at least people who looked like them?* Aside from the fact I find her manner of dress off-putting, she is such a nice person. Look at her husband Mike. If one was to make a comparison, I don't know which of them looks worse. The interesting thing to me is they both present themselves in an intelligent and friendly manner; in fact, it feels as though I have known them for a long time. I'll bet that if a person met them for the first time over the phone, he would probably think they were practicing professionals in some type of business, and would obviously not be swayed by their appearance.

I observed the ant walking toward Vonda. It doesn't seem to have any problem with her. I started to feel uncomfortable and ashamed.

The scriptures state that we should not judge. I didn't think I was judging. From the way I see it, I was simply calling it like it is. However, I noticed using this rationale did not remove the feelings of guilt building inside.

Just as I looked up, I could hear the engine of the bike rev up as Mike down shifted the gears — what a sound it makes. Even though I am concerned about Brad's safety, I'm still affected by this distinctive sound. As I gazed at the two on the bike, I couldn't help but see Mike's ponytail flipping around on the side of Brad's face as Brad was squinting and holding on with a big grin.

"Looks like they're having lots of fun," Vonda finally said.

Mike shut the bike off and quietly coasted up near to where we were standing and stopped. *Boy! This is a nice bike,* I thought, still smitten with the shiny Harley.

"That sure was fun, Dad!" Brad announced, his grin reaching ear to ear.

"Looks like ya made it alright," I countered.

"He was a good passenger," Mike said with a genuine smile.

I thought to myself, *I see him in a whole different context than I did before. As unkempt as he looks, he just seems cool.*

"Gary, take a ride with me." Mike said, pointing to the now-vacant seat behind him.

"No!" I blurted out, surprised, to say the least. "I mean… thanks for the offer though."

"Go on, Gary. I can see it in your eyes — you can't wait," Vonda coaxed.

Well, here I am. Thoughts started rolling into my mind. What excuse could I come up with? *I know it would be really fun, and*

Brad seems to be alright. Why is it okay for my son to be seen with people dressed in this manner, and I'm so hesitant, worrying about what people will think of me?

"Get on, Gary," Vonda said again. It almost felt as though she knew my thoughts, which I hoped she didn't, given all the negative judgements I'd made. Mike grinned and moved forward on the seat so I could get on.

An unanticipated grin immediately crossed my face. "Okay," I finally said and jumped on, the young boy in me winning this time.

Vonda grabbed Brad's hand and walked over next to me on the bike. She touched me on the shoulder and said, "This will be great. It will be the best motorcycle ride you will ever have. I just know it. Brad and I can go inside for some ice cream," which made Brad's big smile reappear.

"Okay, let's go," I said. The responsible father in my head was still scolding me about leaving Brad with a complete stranger.

Mike flipped a switch, stood up on the kick starter, dropped his weight and the engine fired up.

What a rush, I thought. *This is going to be fun.* The chopper appeared to have been a converted 74 Harley Davidson street bike, which is not the year it was produced, but represents the cubic inch displacement of the engine.

Mike turned around and grinned at me. He had those little square sunglasses on which, I now have to admit, would look cool if one found himself a part of this culture. I looked at Mike's ponytail and hoped it wouldn't flutter in my face.

Mike revved up the engine, let up on the clutch, and we started

122

to move.

"You'll probably need to hold on!" Mike shouted, the same instruction he gave my son.

Just so I wouldn't have to hold onto Mike, I found a couple of good grips on the edge of the seat. After a couple of seconds, I assume to give me time to hold on, Mike cracked the throttle. The surge of the 74 caused my hands to instinctively take a tighter grip on the seat. As Mike took the chopper through the gears, I noticed his ponytail start to dance as the bike moved faster. I chastised myself for assuming his ponytail would be greasy and ratted. Instead, it was clean, combed and nicely held together by a black rubber band.

Being a reasonably good observer, my eyes were eventually drawn to the edge of the tattoo on Mike's left arm. I wondered, *why would someone want one of those?* It looked as though it had been there a long time, probably as a young adult. *I wonder if he regrets it.* As Mike went through the gears, I watch our shadows follow us along the edge of the roadway. I could see in the shadow the high handle bars and the hand-filled gloves that were gripping them. It was cool to see the shadow of the extended front forks as they gripped the slender front wheel assembly between them. As the rotation of the spokes caused them to vanish in the shadow, it seemed like the front forks were not connected to the wheel at all. By watching this shadowy image move along the edge of the road, one could possibly think we were good friends, when in reality I am still a bit nervous about this whole experience.

As I continued to stare at the shadows, the image caused me to wonder if Hank had ever ridden a motorcycle in his younger days.

As I thought of Hank, I was intrigued by the fact that he had a childhood like the rest of us, and wasn't born the old, worn-out farmer as he always appeared. I miss old Hank. I was told he had passed away shortly after I had left Montana, but, surprisingly, his passing didn't have much of an effect on me either way at the time, or so I thought.

You see, Hank was my friend. But I am afraid I didn't acknowledge it at the time, nor did I care. As I think about it now, what bothers me the most is the possibility that Hank didn't know I considered him my friend. The thought punched me in the throat.

I remember reading on my mother's refrigerator "A friend is someone who likes you." Though I didn't pay Hank a lot of attention I'm hoping he was aware, by the refrigerator definition, that he was my friend. When I would be at track practice, Hank would always be there watching me. He would encourage me, telling me how good I was and how good I would do at the upcoming track meets. He would talk to the coach and, from time-to-time, run the clock for me when I ran the 100-yard dash. He would be at my football games, as well, with the same kind of positive comments — which we all desperately need at that influential time in our lives. Hank always had positive things to say. When he was around me, I felt that I was his hero. I don't know that I really was, but his encouragement made me feel proud. Hank wore the same old coveralls and hat for as long as I can remember, and right now I would give anything to see him standing by Brad, waiting in those coveralls for me to return.

The noise of Mike's Harley was steady now, and my mind took hold of deep thoughts of the old farmer. Hank was indeed a good man. He was kind to everyone and helped anyone with whom he came in contact. I would see him at the livestock auction sales, where he would sell cattle and calves occasionally. Whenever he would see me, he would always wave from across the arena and eventually would come talk to my dad and me, and he would say something that made me smile.

I remember during the County Fair, our church would have the assignment to help with the clean-up at the livestock show barns. We would have to be there around 6:00am so that we could get the place cleaned before the gates were opened. Along with my dad, I would always see Hank there, and his ritual would be to joke around and make me smile.

What makes me sad is the fact I didn't outwardly appreciate him or let him know how good an influence he was on me. The only thing I could focus on was the fact he didn't seem to have any class; and it was, in part, his and the other farmers' lifestyle why I felt so strongly about leaving my homeland.

Isn't this interesting? Here I am a self-proclaimed redneck, and Mike is likely a certified hippie — at least by my definition — and here we are together. Yes, isn't it ironic, especially when considering our cultural diversity and such; yet I am on the back of his bike, a chopper no less, and a lot closer to him than I thought would ever be comfortable.

"Are ya having fun?" Mike yelled over the roar.

"Ya," I said a little cautiously, not being absolutely sure of the final outcome of this trip. "This is sure a nice bike," I responded after a brief moment of silence. "Did you build it yourself?" I inquired, knowing Mike was a mechanical engineer and would definitely have the know-how.

"Yep; took me about two years." Mike seemed to have a lot of pride in his voice that actually gave me confidence in him. *That's cool,* I thought. *This bike is so pretty with all the chrome and everything polished.* I finally acknowledged his ponytail, which I have unwittingly been fighting for the last couple of miles. I guess because of his personality, I have been able to get past it all. *Well, I didn't see that coming.*

"What the…" Mike blurted out.

"What's the matter?" I asked, peering around his head.

"Hold on," he said, slamming on the brakes, and the bike began to slide. "There's an accident up here." He finally got the bike stopped without any problem. "Looks like somebody is injured and there's nobody around," Mike said.

We both jumped off the bike and ran over to where the accident was. In the crosswalk, lying on the pavement, was a man dressed in a suit with a white shirt and tie. His briefcase had been knocked into the middle of the intersection. There were no vehicles that stopped, so the first thought was a hit-and-run. He seemed to be unconscious, but Mike bent down and checked for a pulse.

"Get my first aid kit from under the seat. Quick!" he instructed me.

I ran to the bike, retrieved the first aid kit, and ran back to Mike. What I saw stunned me. Mike was hunched over the man, giving him mouth-to-mouth resuscitation. I thought…well, I didn't know what to think. Here crouched Mike in his less-than-approachable clothing, forcing his breath into this man, who looks like he probably has enough money in his wallet to cover everything Mike and I own combined. After what seemed an eternity, the man coughed and started to breathe. Mike grabbed his hand and began to ask his patient questions. When his ponytail fell in the man's face, Mike tucked it under his vest.

"Run over to that house and call an ambulance," Mike said, the

urgency in his voice apparent.

I did as instructed, and the ambulance arrived quickly, much to our relief. Mike talked to the attendants, after which they took some information from the victim and loaded him into the ambulance. As I leaned against the ambulance, feeling useless, I noticed Mike was still talking to the victim and holding his hand. My conscience raced back to the truck stop and all those ignorant thoughts about Mike and Vonda. This man, whom I judged so harshly just saved a man's life; he's a true Good Samaritan.

Now I really started to feel awful. Why have I judged Mike and Vonda this way? I don't remember my mom and dad ever telling me that someone like Mike was a bad person. In fact, I recall once when my mother took in a couple of men walking down the street looking for work. My dad gave them a job, and they stayed with us for what seemed to be several weeks. I know times are different now; it's a much bigger risk to do that today, sadly. *I really like Mike*, I thought to myself. *He and his wife are kind people, confident, and seem to be in control of their lives.* I wondered to myself what Hank would have done in this situation, but I knew the answer. He would have done whatever he could to help someone.

After stabilizing the patient, the attendant closed the rear doors, walked to the front and got in. As the ambulance pulled away, I realized Mike had shown as much or more compassion for the man as had the attendants. Mike looked at me and smiled. I could see the concern in his eyes, still present.

"I hope he'll be okay," Mike said.

"I...I think that was a real amazing thing you did there," I responded, clumsily.

At the same moment our eyes dropped to the ground, and Mike asked, "Isn't that what we are supposed to do; look out for each other?"

I nodded. Without saying any more, we slowly walked back to the bike. Mike replaced the first aid kit, after which we climbed on the Harley and started back for the truck stop. We weren't driving as fast as before, and the electricity that was present in the air at the beginning of the ride had vanished.

As we rode along, I began to recall the time when my mother somehow found out about an elderly fellow, sick and near death, I believe. She found an opportunity to help this person out, which consisted of paying him a visit on a weekly basis. He did eventually die, but I will always have those fond memories of her diligent and compassionate service to others. I knew my mother had made that man's passing less lonely.

We finally reached the truck stop and dismounted the bike. When I looked at Vonda, tears came into my eyes that I could not control. I had to turn my head and fight them, so I would not be asked what the problem was — the answer would be awkward, to say the least. Vonda was right; this would be an epic ride.

"I really enjoyed that ride, Mike." It was all I could get out. Mike went on to tell Vonda what we had just experienced, and I was grateful my son was okay, since my ride took longer than expected.

Though I was beginning to feel comfortable with Mike, I was reluctant to call him Hawk; we have only known each other for a short time. I did realize, however, that I had an unanticipated admiration for him.

"Gary, I know I can speak for Mike when I say that we have really enjoyed meeting you and your son," Vonda stated and ruf-

fled Brad's hair. Seems there was a gentle bond formed between them, as well.

As I stared at Vonda and reflected on my previous thoughts, tears welled up in my eyes.

"Are you okay, Gary," Vonda gently inquired.

I didn't say anything.

My eyes glanced at Mike, and an understanding grin came over his face. He put his arm on my shoulder and we all stood there in silence.

"You know, Gary, Vonda and I appreciate the kindness you have shown by you and your son riding on my bike," Mike said genuinely. "We know a lot of folks are uncomfortable with us, especially when we're in our bike get-ups, but we'd sure be honored to call you our friends."

Speechless, I stared at the ground for what seemed several minutes. I saw no ants scurrying now, and no birds singing. It was as though even nature was waiting for my reply.

To break the ice, Vonda walked up to me, pushed Mike's arm from my shoulder and gave me a big hug.

Stammering and stuttering, I said, "I really appreciate the both of you and what you have taught me."

After saying our goodbyes and exchanging telephone numbers, Brad and I slowly walked over to the truck and climbed in. With the image of Mike and Vonda in my mind, I started the engine, tuned in the radio and steered the truck toward the interstate. Looking in the mirror, I could see Mike and Vonda waving, and Brad and I waved enthusiastically in reply. As their images disappeared, I knew in my heart that, because of this experience at the truck stop, my life will likely not be the same. Something inside me was grateful for that.

I steered the truck onto the freeway, carefully lined it up in the center of the traffic lane, and finally relaxed.

"Dad, what is this?" Brad asked, pulling something from his backpack.

"That is an angel, Son. Where did you get it?"

"Mom bought it at the store," he answered, looking closely at the figurine.

"Do you like it?"

"Yeah," he said, now moving it around in the air as someone would with a toy airplane.

"Do you think angels can really fly?" I asked.

Brad answered by shrugging. My little boy seemed sleepy, and I knew I wasn't prepared for a long discussion right now. I was content to just let the question hang in the air.

CHAPTER 9
THE BARN

"I always liked to have Hank watch us when we played. He would always encourage me and made me feel I was a great basketball player even though I knew better."

I was staring out the window, not realizing Brad had awakened and was silently studying the countryside. Suddenly he blurted out, "Dad! Dad! Look!"

Startled, I looked off to the side of the road and noticed a barn on fire. Since we were near an interchange, I decided to pull off and watch for a few minutes.

They're finally getting rid of it, I thought. *It seems like everything having to do with these old farms is going away.* Of course, I don't know whether they are intentionally burning this down or if it has accidentally caught on fire. My thought was no one really cares what happens to these structures or the small farms on which they reside.

I looked thoughtfully at the burning structure; it reminded me of Hank's old, red barn. There are barns like this one scattered all over the western United States. Made me think the farmers must have gotten the building plans from some kind of feed and seed seminar decades ago. Barns have a rather stately look and are a necessary item on the property, if you really want to consider your property a real farm.

I remember when I was younger I would go to Hank's house and play basketball in the hay loft of his barn with one of his sons. There was a basket with a net mounted on a large piece of plywood that hung from the rafters, and worked very well for what we needed. We would have to move the bales of hay around in order to make ourselves a decent court, but it was fun up there. The "out-of-bounds" was essentially the vertical stack of hay, and you didn't need a referee to tell you when you were out, either; doing so would cause you to run or stumble into the bales of hay, and hitting those stacks facing inside the court would result in some significant pain, if you ran into them just right. We would play "Horse," one-on-one, or practice our trick shots for hours at a time, and never seem to get tired. We would eventually hear the barn door slam, followed by slow footsteps coming up the stairs. Hank's tall frame would soon fill the doorway. I always liked to have Hank watch us play, since he would always encourage me, and as with football, he seemed to believe I was a better player than I truly was. *I wonder what kind of athlete Hank would have been, had he been given the chance.*

As the flames continued to weaken and consume the barn's remaining frame, a feeling of sadness built up inside of me. Though I really haven't had much respect for farmers, this barn represents a large part of my short life. Not only did Hank have a barn, but so did we. It was just a different style. It was so old that there was no evidence it had ever been painted.

I remember many times milking our old cow, Suzi, who we considered to be part of our family. She was an old Jersey cow, as I recall — kind of a light yellow color, I guess. She seemed indifferent to us human beings as we could walk up to her, play with her ears and even sit on 'er. I remember one time picking the dried-up skin from the scar of her brand, and she didn't seem to pay much attention.

134

The process of milking consisted of going into the barn and putting some grain in the stanchion, opening the barn door to look outside, whereupon I would spot Suzi, usually in the corral near the barn. Sometimes after I opened the door, she would simply walk in. On other occasions, however, I would have to walk over by her and try to shove her so she would start walking towards the barn. There were a few times, weather permitting, when I would walk out in the pasture and milk her where she stood.

After getting her in the barn and locking her head in the stanchion, I would grab the milk stool and bucket. The milk stool consisted of a couple of two-by-fours, which were cut and nailed together in the form of a "tee." I would take a milk bucket, put it under the cow's bag — that's what we called it — and then carefully place the milk stool in such a position so, when sitting on it, my head would rest in old Suzi's flank, just inside of her hind leg. This posture served a number of useful purposes. It helped prevent Suzi from kicking me or the milk bucket, kept my face further from her dirty tail when she tried to swat me or a fly, and it actually kept me warm in wintertime. It would take me about 10 to 15 minutes to finish the milking.

Any worthwhile conversations consisted of me talking and her listening. During these moments I would sometimes sing or just think about life. Occasionally a cat would wander by and I would squirt her with the milk and she would try to drink it. Or one of my younger sisters would come by and, not being immune to my deadly accuracy, would be sprayed with the milk, accompanied by their screaming. On some occasions, I could squirt the milk up a wall and the cat would run up after it.

On the ceiling about four or five feet from where the old cow stood hung a fly catcher. This was a piece of incredibly sticky tape about two-and-a-half feet long, which flies would land on

and find themselves permanently stuck. The cows didn't seem to appreciate the flies, especially the ones that would bite and cause them to kick, so while the flytrap was unsightly, it was effective. I suppose after much costly research, it was eventually concluded by the agriculture industry flies would be better suited stuck to the unforgiving tape, and would give their all for the simple privilege of spending the remaining hours of their lives immobilized.

After finishing with the milking, I would pour some milk into a bucket with a rubber nipple mounted on the outside near the bottom, which I would use to feed the calves. If there was more than one calf, I would have to get a stick to nudge them back. Ya know, some people are a lot like those calves. If they want something bad enough they will push, shove, and fight for it, no matter what the unintended consequences may be. They're not always respectful of each other, so in a way their behavior isn't much above that of animals, even though humans are purportedly the more civilized creatures.

In our barn, there was a 55 gallon barrel that contained rolled oats, which is what we fed the cows during their milking time. There were a couple of metal buckets in the barrel that my brother and I would use to play basketball. Though the buckets were hard to dribble, we made them work — at least for a few minutes.

As Brad and I watched this old barn continue to burn, an unexpected sadness crept into my heart. For a moment it felt like a part of me was being taken away and no one cared. As I stared, I realized the barn meant more to me than I ever imagined. Before, it was just an old barn that housed my dad's equipment and livestock; but now, it represents the formative years of my life. In a mild state of depression and sadness, I pulled the truck back onto the interstate.

"Why is the barn burning, Dad?"

"I'm not sure, Son." *I'm really not sure.*

CHAPTER 10
DASH LIGHTS

138

"A lot of people live their lives as though warning lights are their only signal; they don't see anything coming until it is often too late."

A s Brad and I drove away from the fire, my eyes were drawn to the dash lights. I noticed there were not many gauges on the instrument panel, but instead just the red warning lights. These lights don't seem as safe or informative as the gauges. I have noticed when a dash light goes on, ironically there is really no warning. The problem is past the point of pre-emptive action. With gauges, the problem will sometimes progress slowly and at least forewarn the driver, if he is observant.

A lot of people live their lives as though warning lights are their only signal; they don't see anything coming until it is often too late. I know a blind man who can play the piano, weed his garden, and will remember anyone he meets simply by hearing their voice. If he were to be put into a physical location he hadn't previously encountered, this man would most likely stumble a few times before he learned the landscape. Conversely, for those of us who can see but refuse to acknowledge what is before us, we have no excuses for a consequential outcome other than we are stubborn, arrogant, or unwilling. Someone once penned the phrase *"To the blind all events are sudden."* I find that phrase far more applicable to those who remain in denial about their circumstances, than those who literally cannot see.

With the onset of automation, we have moved from gauges to dash lights. I have also noticed that vehicles are getting harder to work on. I don't recall a lot of farmers ever taking their equipment to a mechanic for repairs; they just fixed it themselves. I believe technology — while it can be undeniably useful — is taking away people's ability to do things for themselves. So many things are becoming automated.

I remember one time we were leaving church to head home. We had gotten into the car, and Dad tried to start it, but it would not fire. He got some coveralls out of the back and put them over his nice clothes, then he popped the hood and began to work. Sometime later he pulled the distributor out of the engine and showed my brother and me where the gear on it had been stripped. I was impressed my dad could fix nearly anything and I took it for granted. He could repair anything on our property except the television set. I always figured later in life, I would be able to do the same thing; but, I found that being a mechanic did not match my abilities or patience. I understood the principles of how things worked, and though I fancied myself a shade-tree mechanic, I did not have the patience to follow through on a task.

Brad brought my brain to attention when he yelled, "Dad!"

"What?"

"Why is that red light on?" Brad said, pointing to the dashboard. My son was impressing me with his observant nature during this trip.

I shared my gaze between the road and the dash lights. *What now?* I thought. We're miles away from the last town, and the warning light indicates a problem I'm not prepared to deal with. *What am I going to do?* This is annoying and certainly unexpected. After all, this is a nice truck I have paid money to rent. *Don't they take the time*

to maintain their equipment?

"It's a warning light telling us the engine is overheated," I mumbled.

"What are you going to do?" he inquired, wide-eyed.

"I…"

"What's that building over there, Dad?"

With a sigh of relief, I responded, "That's a rest area, Son. We can't drive the truck anymore or it will ruin the engine." I was even more grateful for Brad's skill of observance. I shut off the engine and coasted the truck along the off-ramp until we had come to the rest area parking lot.

"Let's look and see what the problem is." I could smell the antifreeze. I got out, opened the hood and pretending I was a mechanic noticed one of the radiator hoses had sprung a leak. *I could fix this if I had some duct tape,* but I knew I didn't.

"I'm going to move the truck out of the way, then we can walk over and see if we can find a phone," I explained to Brad, but I think we both needed to hear me sound confident.

We found a phone, but it had been vandalized; the phone book was gone, and the cord had been ripped out of the housing. *Why is it necessary to tear things up?* I remember on Halloween, when I was in high school, my buddies and I would get pickup loads of junk and dump it on Main Street. The sheriff's office would send someone out to watch us and it was great fun, but we never vandalized anything and no one got arrested for littering. But, the next day the school superintendent made us clean up the street. It wouldn't surprise me if the superintendent and

the sheriff didn't have that all planned out in advance after the first time.

Staring at the phone in frustration, I surmised one of those carnies or someone of the same caliber has done this.

"Brad, I guess we'll have to wait here and see what happens."

Since the pop machine worked, we both got a can, found a bench to sit on, and decided to wait for a while. This was stressful for me because I like to be in control, and I definitely was not in control here.

As we sat, we saw an old car coming down the freeway. I noticed it was smoking and assumed it was worn-out and burning oil. The driver pulled up near where our truck sat, and parked. A couple of elderly ladies climbed out. They were donning straw hats, different loud-colored pants, a white cotton blouse, and white socks with their shoes. *They must live on a farm,* I mused. Most women on the farm dressed like that whenever they had to go out and work. One of them looked over at us and began to speak.

"Hey, is that your truck?"

"Yes," I responded, a little embarrassed.

"Is there anything we can do for you?" her friend joined.

"The radiator has a leak so I need some duct tape," I replied.

"We don't have any duct tape. Are you guys hungry?" the first woman asked.

"Uh…not really," I responded.

The first thing on a woman's mind, in any case of distress or misfortune, seems to be to quickly determine whether anyone within earshot is hungry.

"I'll bet your son would like some cookies. He looks hungry to me," the second woman chimed in, her friend was nodding in agreement.

Wow, this lady is really nice and doesn't seem to care who we are. Another mental note was written for me to ponder later.

She opened the back door of her car and grabbed a bag of cookies, a couple of bananas and walked over to us. "What is this fine young man's name?"

"Brad," I responded.

"I just bet he would like something to eat and so would you," she said, giving me the maternal eye those grandma-types have. She handed Brad some cookies and a banana and motioned for me to take some as well.

"Thanks," I said. I was hungrier than I realized and took a bite of a cookie, prompting a wink from the kindly woman.

"I guess we will be going now. You young men have a safe journey." She turned and walked with her friend into the building.

"Who were those ladies," Brad asked.

"I don't know, but they are sure nice," I answered, finishing off the cookie. *She reminds me of Hank's wife,* I thought. She was always doing things for other people and very kind to those who came to her house. They were good, honest people you

143

could always trust.

As I sat staring at their car, I recalled all of the good both my mother and father had done for others. How she took in some men looking for a job. She took in an old man with only one hand who lived in our renovated chicken coop for a while. I never knew what happened to him, but I will never forget the service my mother rendered.

I remember the work we had to do on the farm; hauling water to the chickens was no easy task. Bucking and stacking hay bales, changing sprinkler pipes, driving tractor all day were also added to our duties. We would grind grain, a horrible job — very noisy and dusty, and I was thrilled when that job was completed. Though it seemed senseless at the time, I remember picking rocks out of our garden, putting them into potato baskets, and hauling them off. Once a year we had to clean the chicken coop.

In the distance, while Brad and I peeled and ate our bananas, I could see the plume of smoke coming from a tractor, and I could smell the fragrance of the freshly cut hay, a scent that always reminds me of home.

I scanned the freeway and noticed a car coming into the rest area. As it approached, I could tell it wasn't in very good shape. One of the side windows had a piece of cardboard in it, apparently to replace the broken glass. The hubcaps were gone. (I think they are always the first part to go when preventive maintenance goes away.) I noticed the car was kind of leaning to one side, like a spring was broke as it pulled into a parking space. The door opened and a short man exited the car, holding a cigarette in one hand and a cane in the other. Watching, I noticed he was limping and he looked rough. As he walked by Brad and me towards the restroom, we stared at each other, not speaking but offering a smile and a nod.

I noticed oil dripping from beneath his car. From my perspective, the car was a sign this guy was poor, as there was no part of his bucket-of-rust that appeared to not have had any work done over the years.

After a time, he came out of the restroom and walked towards us. As he came closer, I felt I needed to say something, but here was an internal fight in my mind; I don't feel comfortable initiating conversations when it isn't completely obvious the other party wants to talk.

"Hi," I finally blurted out. For me, waiting for the response could be compared to lighting a cherry bomb and throwing it into the weeds; I'm kind of tense until it goes off.

"Howdy," he returned. I was relieved he said something. "That your truck," he asked, acknowledging the U-Haul with a nod.

"Yes. It has a leak in the radiator hose and most of the antifreeze has drained out," I explained, feeling deflated. "If I had some duct tape, I would be back on the road already," I resigned, hoping this man wouldn't judge me as incompetent.

He took a drag from the cigarette, squinted and coughed. It looked like the cigarettes had taken their toll on him. I understand they are very addictive and it takes a lot of courage and self-determination to stop. It is sad to me, to watch people become crippled and killed by such a dispensable habit.

"Where are ya headed?" he asked.

"Movin' west."

"You going to a new job, or ya just escaping eastern Idaho?" he responded with a short cackle.

"New job," I said, smiling at his wit.

Reaching for my hand he introduced himself. "My name is Larry, and yours?"

"Gary," I replied, not knowing for sure what to think.

"Nice to meet you, Gary," he stated. "So yer goin' to a new job, eh?" he repeated, flicking the stack of ashes from his cigarette.

"Yes, I am," somewhat reluctant to continue with the conversation.

"Is this your boy?" Larry asked, giving a friendly wink to Brad.

"Yes. This is Brad," I replied, staring at Larry's boots. They were the boots the carnies and bikers tended to wear.

"May I sit down?" he asked. I wasn't sure why he needed my permission, but found it polite of him to ask.

"Of course," I said, motioning for him to sit on the bench with us. He sat down and leaned his cane on the bench beside him. He was a casual man, and seemed to lighten up compared to when he first went into the restroom. Or maybe I had.

We sat there for a few minutes watching people go in and out of the restroom. After a few moments passed, a newer, shiny Cadillac pulled up and entered a parking space. Not surprisingly, the running engine expressed itself quietly.

In a backwards sort of way, the running car reminded me of

Hank's pickup, which essentially had no mufflers. People would always tease him about it, but he didn't seem to care. It was noisy, but in an interesting way it was Hank's trademark; we always knew it was him a mile up the road before reaching the Colonel's store.

The car was a two door, hard top, and a pretty blue, which seemed to catch everyone's attention; well, ours, anyway. We watched in silence to see who would appear.

After sitting for a few moments, an elderly couple got out of the car. They had a little poodle with them that seemed to be the focus of their attention. It was apparent to me, not only because of the Cadillac but also their manner of dress, they were very wealthy. I thought to myself, *these people seem affluent. I wonder what it's like to be rich like that. Wonder if they ever had to work hard like I did.*

As we all looked on, the couple walked along the sidewalk toward the rest area. As they approached us, I thought they would offer a greeting, but they did not. Their little dog walked over and relieved itself on Larry's cane, and I expected a scolding from its owners. Nothing was said — they simply waited for the poodle to finish its business, then continued to walk in silence towards the building.

"I guess the dog didn't like my cane," Larry finally stated, a hint of annoyance in his tone.

How can these people be so rude? They looked like they had a lot of class. It is one thing to have a dog do that, but why didn't they apologize? My eyes were drawn to the cane, to Larry's boots, and then to the shoes of those who had just insulted Larry. I would have believed it was an unintentional oversight on their part, had I not just witnessed them watching their dog complete his task.

"I have some duct tape in the car," Larry stated, breaking the silence. "Let's see if we can get the hose fixed." He slowly stood up, which seemed hard for him to do. He grabbed his cane and wiped if off on the grass.

With the duct tape he retrieved from his car in hand, we walked over to the truck in silence.

"It's that bottom hose with the leak in it," I said, popping the hood and peering into the engine. Larry laid his cane down and climbed underneath the truck to see what needed to be done. "You know, you don't need to do this; I can handle it," I said, hoping my gratefulness wasn't masked by condescension.

"I don't mind. It's not the first time I've worked on a truck. This should be easy," he said, pulling a knife from his pocket. Larry put the end of the duct tape on the radiator hose and started to wrap it.

"Yep, ya got a pretty good leak here. I suspect most of yer antifreeze is gone, my friend. It's a good thing you paid attention to that warning light, or you would have fried the engine." *Why would he call me his friend? He doesn't even know me,* I mulled over in my head.

"Wonder how many engines would be spared if everyone heeded the warning lights," I said, grinning. "I know people who would drive until the red light burned out before they would ever stop the engine.

"Or until the engine shut itself off!" Larry quipped, and we both laughed.

Staying on the topic of warnings, "Don't you think it was foolish for those people near Mount Saint Helens not to leave when they were given the warning?" I asked. "And how 'bout all the warnings

148

in the Bible. Have you ever thought maybe some of those old parables apply to us, in today's world?"

Larry sat the duct tape and his knife on the ground and laid there looking up at the engine.

He thoughtfully responded, "Yes, I believe they apply to me."

Curious as to why he singled himself out, I asked, "Why do you say that?"

"When I was younger, I wasn't a very good person. I used to drink quite a bit and I wasn't very nice to people." Larry looked embarrassed, and things felt awkward. "You see, Gary, I had a big problem with stealing. I was a real good pick-pocket. In the back of my mind I always knew it was wrong, but it was such a rush to steal something." He pondered his comments momentarily. "My life was a mess."

"What made you change?" I asked, genuinely curious.

"Met a guy who became my friend and he set a good example for me."

"So…," I paused, hesitating to complete my original question and opted for one less intrusive. "Do you always help strangers like this?"

"Isn't that what we're supposed to do?" he replied.

I sat in silence not knowing what to say, and realizing this was the second time on this trip I had been presented with that comment. The first was Mike after he had provided aid to the hit-and-run victim. The way I'd always seen things, people like Larry and Mike would be *getting* help instead of *giving* it.

"You like mechanic work?" I thoughtfully asked.

"Yep, I enjoy the challenge," Larry replied, finishing up the task at hand.

"I don't have the patience for it. Seems like things don't go back together like they are supposed to," I mumbled.

"What do you do for work?" Larry asked.

"Civil Engineering."

"Is that what your new job is going to be?"

"It is," I said proudly. "I've been hired as the City Engineer for a small town west of here."

"That sounds interesting," Larry responded, wiping his hands on his pants.

"So, where do you work?" I asked. I wanted to be able to convey my friendliness as he had. It didn't seem like he had a steady job, or he would have put money into his transportation. But I didn't want to make any assumptions.

"I was a mechanic for a while, but I hurt my leg so I had to quit. Then I got a job working for a carnival, where I have been most of my life."

"Oh." My reaction made an audible thud in my ears. Larry seemed to sense my uneasiness. As I stared at the radiator cap in my hands, emotions began to stir inside me.

This guy is a carnie. My thoughts raced back to the experiences I had with those people. They looked rough and mean, and I hat-

150

ed to be around them. I began to feel sad, as though I had betrayed Larry and I didn't even really know who he was. I instantly recalled, with painful accuracy, the thoughts I had and the things I said about carnies.

I sat speechless as I watched Larry putter with the engine. Again, he must have sensed something by the way I stopped talking.

"Do you have a problem with people who work in carnivals?" Larry asked, taking the cap from me and replacing it on the radiator. For a few seconds, the blood in my face ran cold. I didn't know what to say.

After a time trying not to show my hand, I said, quietly, "Yes, I used to." I struggled inside; I knew I was not telling the whole truth. My conscience was screaming at me. *Tell him how you really feel,* it said. I knew I had to say something quickly or the lie would be obvious.

I stumbled over my words at first. "I…I have had problems with people who worked at carnivals ever since I can remember."

"How come?" the mechanic inquired, wiping his forehead with his sleeve.

"Well…" I was becoming very uncomfortable with where this conversation was going. Sometimes the truth is hard. I remember when I was in high school, and the school bus I rode stopped at a dairy to pick up some students. We, of course, would make comments about the smell. Later, I found myself in the school superintendent's office. He asked me if I had made any negative comments about the smell of the dairy and I confessed that I had. My parents told me sometime later the

151

superintendent was impressed with my honesty. That didn't console me much.

"Is it because you consider them low-lifers?"

The question jerked me back into reality. "Ya. I guess."

"Well, Gary," he started, "at least yer honest." There was an uncomfortable silence for a time, then Larry spoke again, "Ya know, Gary, I have to admit there are some really bad people that work at carnivals. Do you know a lot of folks call us carnies?"

"Yes." Of course I did — I was one of them. There was a profound silence while Larry inspected the engine.

"You know, it doesn't seem like you ever worked for a carnival," I mentioned, to see what he would say.

"You mean as a carnie?"

"Ya." We both laughed, though mine was nervous energy. I noticed Larry was getting serious.

"Gary, I have learned that you can't judge people as a group. I have done it my whole life, but it never seems to be very accurate."

I thought to myself, *I judge people all of the time.* I climbed down off of the truck and handed Larry his cane. We walked back to the bench, and Larry motioned for Brad to come over by him.

"What grade are you in, Brad?"

"Second," my son replied, quite proud of himself.

"Is your teacher nice?"

"Yes! She lets us play games and she reads to us if we're good, but I am getting a new teacher" Brad responded with a smile.

"Well, that's good to hear. Brad, bring me that piece of wood there, please, and I'll carve something for ya," Larry offered.

Brad jumped up, trotted over, picked up the wood and handed it to Larry, who pulled out his knife and began to carve. As I watched the process, I noticed that his knife was very nice, having a pearl handle and all.

"Wow, where'd you get that knife?" Brad asked. He had noticed it, as well.

"I got it at a carnival. I made quite a bit of money at my booth one day, so my boss gave it to me."

"I have a pocket knife, too, but it's not pretty like that one," Brad explained, admiring the knife.

"I would give it to ya, but ya probably shouldn't have a knife like this, until yer older," Larry explained. "I have an idea, though." Larry stood up and walked over to his car with the aid of his cane, retrieved a small box, and returned to the bench.

"Here ya go, Brad." He handed Brad the box, and Brad stared at it for a few seconds, unsure of what to do. "Go ahead and open it," Larry urged.

Brad opened the box and found a little battery-powered 4-wheeler. "Cool!" my son squealed, cradling the toy in his hands. "Do you have a boy my age, too?"

"Nope, I don't. It's yours, Brad," Larry said, smiling brightly.

"Thanks a lot!" Brad said in return. I was proud of my son's manners.

"You're welcome, Brad. I'd be real proud if you'd do something nice for someone else one day." Larry winked and tussled Brad's hair.

We sat there for a bit longer, watching people come and go from the rest area, while Larry focused on carving. I thought of all the times I have had people help me, not only with tasks, but with just being a friend so I would have someone to hang out with. Although I'm a little reserved, I do like people and I don't like to always be alone.

"Well, here ya go, Brad," Larry said, reaching over and handing Brad an over-sized, wooden fish hook, complete with the barbs and the eye for the fishing leader.

"Thanks," Brad said, excited. "Thanks a lot!"

"You bet, Brad. Guess I oughta get going. Hope that duct tape holds for the rest of yer trip, Gary. I'll give someone a call 'bout runnin' some antifreeze out here to ya."

"Thanks a lot for helping us and keeping us company, Larry. It sure was nice of you," I said sincerely, reaching out to shake his hand.

"You bet." Larry walked over and got into his car. As he started the engine, a big puff of blue smoke bellowed from the exhaust pipe. He rolled down the window, raising his voice over the engine, "Doesn't say much for a mechanic, does it?" and he began driving away, waving once more out his window.

As Larry pulled away towards the on-ramp, I couldn't help but

think, *Larry is truly one of God's angels — a real person who came to help me.* I sat on the bench thinking about Larry and all the things he said and did while he was here.

"Dad, that guy was nice to us, huh," Brad commented, admiring his new gifts from the friendly stranger.

Caught up in my own thought, I finally responded, "Yes. He was, Son. Very nice."

I wondered if I had ever been like Larry to someone else. The part that bothers me the most, I suppose, is not just knowing, but being very aware of the really great things both my parents did for other people. Some people aren't even raised to be kind to each other, much less to provide service. I certainly had a good example. I suppose on the great Judgment Day, I won't have much of an excuse for not being a decent human being. Nope, I don't suspect I will be highly rewarded for servitude to my neighbors.

I can't really say why I chose the path I'm on, although I do recall Dad loaning some of his equipment out, and it would usually come back all beat up. I think watching this when I was a child made me selfish, something I have always struggled with. To this day I am happy to help someone, but I am not excited about loaning my stuff. I remember lending my lawnmower to a friend, and it came back trashed. I shouldn't have been surprised, as his house resembled the returned lawnmower. Yes, it still ran, but it had not been taken care of, was all dirty and greasy, and — much to my dismay — the plastic orange handle cover to the throttle was missing. I would always spray off the mower and frequently clean the grease from the engine, so it was frustrating to see my nearly-pristine mower in that condition. Now I would almost rather *give* my stuff to someone, expecting it not to return at all (although that thought isn't any

more gratifying) than to loan it out and have it returned in very poor condition.

Wouldn't I be in a sorry position if nobody was willing to help me out today? Or what if Mike had been unwilling to offer assistance to the accident victim? I pondered that thought for a long while. For whatever reason, I wasn't in a hurry to get back on the freeway. Brad was content playing with his new toys, so I grabbed a bottle of juice from the vending machine and relaxed.

CHAPTER 11
COVERALLS

158

"These old guys seem like they've been friends forever."

"Look at that old truck!" Brad shouted. I looked up and saw an old Ford pickup coming into the rest area. It wasn't in very good shape, but from what I could tell it sounded good; the engine seemed tight and didn't appear to be burning any oil.

As the truck approached, it reminded me of the problems I've had with vehicles and equipment. As a young husband, I remember going to school when it was so cold I had to carry the battery of our car into the entryway of our apartment to keep it warm. I would be able to start it then, so I could take my wife to work. It seems like only the poor have to worry about auto maintenance. Ever see any vehicles around rich people's homes, with the hoods up and no wheels on them? Seems the rich just trade 'em in when the new ones come out. The rich seem to get it all. Joyce would say, "You seem to think the grass is always greener on the other side, Gary. Money might make their lives a little easier, but that doesn't mean they don't have big problems."

As an engineer, I will probably never be rich, but I don't think I will have to live the way the farmers I knew appeared to have lived. Their greener grass was more like hay.

The pickup pulled up in front of the rest area, offering me a front-row view of it. The paint was chipped and faded; the left bumper was bent down. I thought it strange he would park that piece of junk right in front of the building, where everyone can see it. After the engine was shut off, it made a loud report like a firecracker.

The truck door groaned and pinched as it opened, and a large man in coveralls got out with just a bit of trouble. He looked around and gave a slight nod when he spotted us. *He's a farmer. No wonder his pickup looks like that.*

At this same time, an elderly gentleman walking along the sidewalk towards the restroom said with a grin, "Anybody survive that wreck?"

To my surprise, the farmer replied, without being defensive or missing a beat, "Na, she's my huntin' truck. Ma don't let me take the car when I'm runnin' errands." The farmer approached the elderly man, introducing himself with a handshake, "Ed Reynolds."

Accepting the farmer's hand, the old man returned, "Gilbert Southerland."

I didn't mean to eavesdrop, but their conversation was within earshot. *This is funny. These old guys seem like they've been friends forever.* I remember when I was young, people of their era were always friendly with each other, as though they had bonded before they ever met. I could only attribute it to simpler times.

"Good to meet ya, Gilbert. Looks like yer out enjoyin' your retirement money," Mr. Reynolds quipped.

"Eh, figure it's not enough money for the kids to fight over, so I guess I'll do the economy a favor, and spend it on myself and the wife." Both men chuckled.

The farmer reminds me of Hank, wearing coveralls and an old

hat. The two men spoke for several minutes as Brad and I looked on, and with another handshake parted ways.

I hadn't closed the hood on the U-Haul yet, and while a number of well-to-do people walked by us, none stopped to inquire if we needed some help. I became aware it was starting to get dark, and we should probably get back on the road before we are missed and Joyce begins to worry.

As I stood up, Mr. Reynolds acknowledged our rental truck. "That your movin' rig?" he asked.

"Yes, sir," I replied, sounding like an adolescent boy. I'm so intimidated when strangers address me with confidence, as Mr. Reynolds seems to have. A lot of people seem to have more confidence than do I. I can be pretty confident when I am around people I know, but with strangers I am pretty shaky. I'm hoping with age I will be able to overcome this.

Mr. Reynolds walked over to where Brad and I were sitting. "S'the matter with it?"

"The bottom radiator hose sprung a leak and lost the antifreeze. There was a guy who stopped and helped us fix the leak with some duct tape, but he didn't have any antifreeze." A little embarrassed, I broke eye contact and looked at the ground.

"I'll bet the three of us can get 'er fixed. What's yer name, Son?"

"Gary Haley."

"Nice to meet you, Gary," reaching his hand out. "Ed Reynolds," he stated, shaking my hand.

I noticed his hand was big and as I gripped it, it easily conveyed strength. Most people I have seen his age — and he looked pretty old — didn't seem to be very strong. It was evident he has worked hard for a long time.

"Is this your boy?" he asked, smiling.

"Yes, this is Brad."

"Considering what those rigs are used for, seems to be in good shape," Mr. Reynolds announced. "That hose should be an easy fix. Why don't you come with me? You guys hungry?"

"Yes," Brad blurted out, without hesitation. Now I felt worse. He probably thinks I don't take care of my son.

"Let's see if we can find something," Mr. Reynolds said motioning us to follow him.

It seems like I should call him Mr. Reynolds. I don't feel comfortable enough to call him by his first name. I guess that's what I'll do.

We walked over to his pickup. I noticed it was a 1966 Chevy, almost identical to the one I used to own. Like most '66 Chevys, the gearshift was on the floor. I let Brad get in first, while Mr. Reynolds climbed in the driver's side.

"Just scoot over here, Brad, and you can help me drive," our new acquaintance instructed.

While I was quite surprised by my willingness to trust so many new people on this trip, he seems to be another nice guy. He also seems to have a lot of patience with kids. Normally, when I'm with other adults I don't pay much attention to children, someone else's or mine. I'm not proud of my hang-up with this; I can be selfish,

wanting the attention to be on me, and not somebody else.

I made sure Brad was buckled in, then I shut the door and stared at the dashboard.

"Okay, Brad, see this gearshift?" the farmer asked, and Brad nodded. "See the 'R'? You push it clear to the right and pull it down, and we'll be able to back 'er out of here."

Mr. Reynolds turned the key and started the truck, while Brad grabbed the gearshift knob with both hands and pulled as hard as he could, shifting into reverse. I was surprised how well the motor sounded. It sure ran a lot smoother than the Chevy I used to have.

"Why do you have such an old pickup?" Brad asked.

"I've been working on it awhile, to restore it. It's my 'project pickup'," he explained. I smiled, appreciating his goal.

As we pulled towards the highway, we drove past our truck. "Do you think it will be okay, Dad? I mean, all our stuff is in there," Brad asked, concerned.

"She'll be fine," Mr. Reynolds said. "We don't have a lot of crime 'round here." Brad seemed to relax after that.

"I think we'll go down to the store and get a new hose and some clamps along with that antifreeze. I'd hate for ya to be caught in the dark if that duct tape don't hold."

This guy sure is being nice to us, I thought, and again reminded myself I probably wouldn't have done the same for another traveling stranger. *I need to work on changing that,* I thought, and set a goal in my mind.

"Ok, Brad are you ready? When I push on the clutch, I want you to shift it in to 3rd, right there," Mr. Reynolds instructed, pointing out where third gear was. "Ya got it?"

"Yes, sir!" Brad responded, with a grin. I was proud of Brad's willingness to try something new.

As the truck moved along, I became aware of how well the interior looked. The dashboard and floor mats were all clean and new, and someone had redone the upholstery. There were no scratches in the glass covering the dashboard. Everything seemed to be new and without blemish. *This truck really is fancy. Doesn't look like much on the outside, but the inside is immaculate.*

I think this is backwards from what humans often display. A lot of people offer a better impression outwardly than who they are on the inside. Mr. Reynolds doesn't look like much on the outside, so maybe he is great on the inside, where it really counts. There are a lot of props in this world, a lot of glitter, glitz and shiny paint, that when peeled away often reveals unpleasant innards. In my years, I have noticed there are a lot of people who have great paint on the outside and are really flashy, but when they are completely exposed, there is no substance in their character; it's all phony. They can't look you in the eye. I've met a lot of professional people who seem to have similar personality traits. They all have something to sell, and for some, their livelihood depends on their ability to present a shiny exterior.

"Let's pull into this service station. Looks like they might have what we need." Mr. Reynolds turned on the signal and within a few feet parked his truck. "You guys want a soda pop?"

"Sure," Brad and I responded together.

"Your truck looks really nice," I mentioned. "May I have a look

164

at the engine?"

"Absolutely!" Mr. Reynolds answered, and popped the hood. I could tell that he was excited to show me his hard work.

As I said, I've never been much of a mechanic, but I have developed an appreciation for automobile engines. I remember a friend had a Mustang with a modified 428. With the high compression engine and the effects of the high-lift cam, it sounded great. However, deceptively written on the cowling was the number 390, so by the outward appearance one would likely believe the car was nowhere close to being as powerful as it really was. My buddy and I would ride around during noon hour, baiting people to race. Not only was it a big block V8, it was hopped up to race. Cocky as we were, we would pull up to a traffic signal alongside another "hot car." Once we'd get eye contact, each driver would rev their engines. When the light turned green, clutches were dumped and we would blow them away. It was only luck that prevented us from getting a ticket. After a short race, and with shock and awe, the other driver would usually stop us and inquire as to what was under the hood.

Mr. Reynolds walked around to the front of his truck and braced the hood. "Watcha think, Gary?" he proudly inquired.

"It is *incredible*," I responded with a genuine smile.

As Mr. Reynolds stood there with his hand on the hood, the clean, black spark plug wires that connected the plugs to the distributor cap caught my eye. The air cleaner and the other engine components were clean and shiny. I noticed all the electrical systems, the firewall, and all the parts I could see were newly painted. Though it appeared everything under the hood was stock, it was impressive to gaze upon.

"Are ya good? I'm getting thirsty," the farmer announced.

"Me too," my son agreed.

Mr. Reynolds pulled the hood down enough to release the springs and let it fall with a slam that only the hood of a '66 Chevy can produce.

A soda pop sounded good. It reminded me of when my dad would stop to get gas when we were traveling or on an errand; he would always ask if we wanted a soda pop. I have noticed that older people refer to them as soda pops, while we "youngsters" just refer to them as pop.

We all turned to walk into the store. On our way in, I could smell the odor of the gas station. They all smell the same, of gasoline, grease, and oil. There was a burly man standing behind the counter, resting his large frame on the glass case. His friendly smile was contagious.

"Gentlemen, what can I do ya for?" he asked as we approached. I have heard this saying many times and always wondered why people found it clever.

With a smile, Mr. Reynolds looked behind himself as though the parts man was talking to someone else. "'Gentlemen' is kind of a loose term, is it not?"

"I suppose," returned the parts man, smirking. The name embroidered in red on his work coveralls said "Marv."

"Say, we need a bottom radiator hose, a couple of hose clamps and a gallon of antifreeze for a 1977 Chevrolet, 350 V8 truck," Mr. Reynolds listed. "Let's buy a round of soda pops and snacks for these fine men, and for you, too. These kids are moving and the

rig they rented decided to puke up all the antifreeze."

After jotting down our order, Marv left for a few moments and came back with the pops, snacks, and our parts for the truck.

"That comes to $8.48; an even eight dollars for the items, and forty-eight cents for the Governor of our great state."

"Will ya accept one of these worthless Federal Reserve notes?" Mr. Reynolds quipped with a grin.

"Sure, if you'll take one back for change," Marv kept the joke going, handing him a paper dollar and some coins.

"Why'd he say they're worthless, Dad?" Brad asked, quite con-fused.

Not completely understanding myself what the farmer meant, I answered, "I'm not sure, Son. Guess we'll have to get Mr. Reynolds to explain."

"Take this dollar bill and I'll fill ya in later," Mr. Reynolds said, handing me the dollar bill.

I took the bill and went to put it in my pants pocket, but caught myself. Since it wasn't mine, I decided to put it in my shirt pocket, instead.

Marv then handed Mr. Reynolds a sack and a receipt. "If you can't fix 'er, come back and I'll get someone to help ya," burly Marv said. "And that'll be my contribution to your move," he stated, again sharing his friendly smile.

"Thank ya, kindly," Mr. Reynolds said and waved as he turned

toward the door.

"Thanks, Marv. You've been a big help," I chimed in, not wanting to seem ungrateful or unrefined. I instructed Brad to say a thank-you as well, passing down the manners my mother instilled in me when I was a young boy.

CHAPTER 12
RALPH

"As many as there was when I bought it," came the reply.

As I had stood in the gas station, staring at the counter and periodically glancing at Marv, I realized he reminded me of a friend I met at a nursing home. Don't know why, but my mind began to drift back to the time when I visited the old gentleman regularly.

I recall I found the nursing home to be a very interesting place. Set back in the trees on the side of a hill, was a three-story building constructed of a white-brick exterior, and surrounded by a parking lot. The entryway was covered with a canopy, offering protection to visitors and residents from the weather.

I remember one visit specifically. When entering the building, I was blasted by that awful, pungent smell typical of any nursing home or healthcare facility. They say it's the result of a sanitizer; nonetheless, the odor is foul, but in a strange way seems appropriate for the surroundings. As I walked along, I was greeted by a wooden statue that slightly annoys and offends me. It sports a stupid-looking smile, somewhat resembling a clown, and I think in a subtle way degrades the residents for whom I never used to care. I've wanted to take an ax to it (an unlikely possibility), but I would agree, instead, that its ultimate destiny would find its rightful place at the bottom of a landfill, or turned into ashes by someone who has an extra match for which he has no need.

Further down the hall, I found two ladies in wheelchairs. One has lost a leg and greets me with a smile, her face thin and drawn; but she appears happy. The other asked me if I would help her, but I could tell by looking into her eyes her thoughts were now distant and her words on a continuous loop, so I continue my journey down the hall. *What a sad ending to life,* I thought. I made a mental note to myself that, should I ever be placed in a facility like this, *any* way I could leave it would be a *good* way. As I passed by a doorway to a room, there was an old man lying on his bed, crying continually, "Nurse, Nurse!" Concerned, I stopped by the nurses' station to inform them of his pleas. They told me he was in a constant hallucinating state, that he wasn't even conscious of his actions. So, no one came to his aid. *How do they know he isn't conscious of his situation? What a dreadful existence.*

I continue heading for room 316 where my friend, Ralph, resides. When I reach it, I perk up and walk in. The room has two beds, and I notice the one near the door is not occupied. I wondered to myself if that individual had passed on. Ralph's living space is at the far end of the banal room with sterile white walls, graying floor, and bulk-purchased linens. Ralph has gray, curly hair and beard, and dark eyebrows looming over his still-bright eyes. You can tell he had been a fairly good looking guy in his younger days, but, sadly, he is a shadow of his former self. Walking over to where he sat, I put my hand on his shoulder gently, not wanting to startle him.

"Hi, Ralph."

He didn't acknowledge me; he was preoccupied with a well-used dictionary that appears to have been in his possession for a long time. The cover is gone and the edge of the pages are tattered and torn. He was infatuated with words, and kept a tablet on the bed where he wrote down words he found intriguing. Ralph was especially fond of words with double letters, different meanings, or

the like. I suppose this exercise kept his mind active. His hands shake along with his head and neck. At times he shakes more violently than others, and sometimes he doesn't shake at all. He is leaning over the bed, and I peer over his shoulder. Surprisingly, his penmanship is good; no matter how hard he shakes, he can still write well enough so I can read it.

Uninvited, I sat on the other end of the bed where I leaned against the wall in a slouched posture, my legs dangling over the edge. I noticed his pencil was dull so I sat forward, letting him know I would sharpen it and the others lying on the table. After, I replaced the pencil in his hand, leaned back against the wall and looked across the room.

Glancing around, my eyes fell on a table where there was a puzzle, partially put together, along with several country western CDs. I spot a few puzzle pieces lying on the floor and it is apparent, with his hands shaking as they do, handling the puzzle pieces was difficult for him. Further to my left was a row of bowling trophies. As trophies go, they were probably not worth any more than what someone might pay at a typical garage sale. However, to Ralph, it was obvious they were very important; especially considering the fact they represented a significant time in Ralph's life when he was talented and able to accomplish great things in sports. I imagine they added to the identity Ralph wanted to preserve. Across the bed from me is a slide rule with a nice case he used years before. I knew Ralph had a brilliant mind, manifested by the things he displayed in his room, and through the topics we had discussed. Higher on the wall was mounted a bulletin board to which several pictures of attractive women were attached — some movie stars and such. The poses were not immodest, but simply attractive and, I guessed, reminded Ralph of his prime years.

To get Ralph's attention, I put my head closer to the dictio-

nary. He looks at me with some surprise and stares at me for a couple of seconds.

"What words are you looking for?" I asked.

It was often difficult to understand Ralph because the shaking caused his voice to tremble. For some odd reason, I always found myself talking too loudly. Ralph refocused his eyes on the dictionary.

"Here is a word with two Ks. Knock-kneed," he finally muttered and turned to write down his great find.

I thought to myself, *this seems really meaningless for someone with such a powerful mind to be concerned about. He spends an inordinate amount of time with this dictionary.*

It seemed Ralph's mind became lucid again. "How are you doin'?" Ralph inquired.

"I am good," I responded. "How many words do you think you know?"

The elderly man responded, looking down his nose and squinting at me, "Oh…about 35,000… I guess…" then was interrupted mid-sentence.

"Time for dinner, Ralph," came a voice from behind us. I turned to see a nurse with a nice smile. I'm guessing her inflection was intended to make the meal seem more palatable.

"Are you nice to all the residents here, or just Ralph?" I tactlessly inquired. *Well, that sounded bad,* I scolded in my mind.

"I try to be nice to all of them," the nurse replied. Ralph looked

at me like *I* should be the one utilizing the room.

"Since you have company, Ralph, do you want me to bring your food in here?" she asked.

Looking at me, Ralph asked, "If you're going to stay, I'll eat here."

"Yes, I'll stay," I replied.

The nurse left the room, and Ralph looked back at his dictionary.

"How many words are in that dictionary?" I asked.

"As many as there was when I bought it," came the reply. I had to laugh. *What a great comeback.* Ralph was really an extraordinary guy, and had such a great sense of humor.

"My roommate died," he blurted out.

I didn't know what to say. There was an uncomfortable silence in the room for a few moments. I was glad the man was finally at peace; he seemed so miserable, and shared his misery with Ralph. The man would go in long streaks of yelling out in such a manner that it was hard to hear when Ralph and I would talk, and to be honest, it caused me some anxiety. I wondered why they didn't put the gentleman in a room with someone with a similar condition. Ralph had enough trouble trying to deal with his own troubles, much less with the noisy background. I remember on one occasion Ralph's roommate became so loud we couldn't hear each other talk. Finally, out of frustration, Ralph startled me with a nonsensical yell of his own. I felt a little embarrassed, but it seemed to work — his roommate became silent. But on this visit, I think Ralph missed his roommate or he would not have mentioned his passing.

"Aren't you excited to go to the next world?" I asked. I was curious about his perspective on what happens after we die.

"You mean the happy hunting ground?" he said, with a crooked finger pointing up.

"Yes."

He didn't answer.

I noticed a stack of National Geographic magazines in a stand close to the wall. I moved across the room and reached down to retrieve one.

"You read these?" I question, flipping through the magazine.

"Yep."

I was not surprised at all that Ralph read these popular, informative publications. He had a very deep understanding of many things, and seemed to be well-organized, too. There was a cabinet full of country CDs, at least a couple hundred of them.

"Someone accidently took these magazines and put them out front. So I had to get them back," he explained, tapping on the magazine with his shaking and age-spotted hands. On the front cover of the issue I held was a picture of an Egyptian pyramid.

"How do you think they built these?" I asked, genuinely interested in his knowledge.

"They had to move stones that weighed 200 tons, 100 miles," he responded.

"How would they ever move them so far?"

"I have no idea." I could tell by looking into Ralph's eyes as he spoke, he is very intelligent. He had far more knowledge packed away than what he displayed to me.

"Ralph, did you go to college?" I ask.

"Yes." I appreciated his quick, curt answers.

"What did you major in?"

"Mathematics. You see that can?" he asked, pointing to an old tin can on a shelf. I nodded. "You can use Calculus to determine the least amount of material to be used in the can, while maintaining a certain volume." I could tell he was proud of his knowledge.

Yes I know, Ralph, I thought to myself, although I believed he probably knew this subject even better than I, an engineer.

"Here it is, Ralph," said the nurse finally arriving with his meal. The tray was a typical faded pink plastic, multi-sectioned container, presenting an unremarkable meal. I'm sure I didn't do a very good job of hiding my expression, seeing the unappealing blobs in each section. The nurse sat the tray on the table and left the room.

"Ralph, listen to this and see what you think — humor me for a moment. I have read where it states a comet or comets have come dangerously close to the earth. When this happened there was an electrical discharge between the earth and the passing comet in the form of a large lightning bolt. When this occurred, it changed the gravitational or magnetic attraction of the earth. They say that the earth's gravity had a lot less attraction before this happened. Could that not possibly account for how they moved those large stones?" I finished my statement, feeling I had posed a credible scenario.

Ralph looked at me, rolled his eyes and shook his head — intentionally, this time. He grabbed his tablet and pencil, rapidly turned a page with his shaking hand, and drew a pyramid and a ramp. He then illustrated a stone mounted on some logs and people pulling the stone up the ramp with ropes. As quickly as he picked up the tablet, he laid it back down. Everything he did with his hands, he did quickly, despite the shaking.

"There! That is how it was done," Ralph said with finality, and firmly put the pencil on his table. Being put in my place, I slowly laid the magazine on the bed.

He started to eat. Out of politeness, I discontinued our conversation. Even though his appearance and condition were sad and unkempt, I noticed my respect for him matched that of my college professors. I had really grown to love Ralph, and considered him my friend. For reasons we don't understand, our perceived dignity is sometimes taken from us in our later years, but in my mind Ralph had retained his.

As I think of Ralph, my mind wanders back to Hank. *There are some parallels here*, I thought to myself. *Hank was crippled socially, while Ralph was crippled physically; Hank was very capable in what he knew, Ralph was also very capable in what he knows; Hank liked me and I think Ralph liked me, as well; by appearance, Hank was easy to misjudge, and Ralph would be, as well; and most importantly, they have both unintentionally taught me great lessons in life.*

Ralph finished his meal. "How was it?" I asked, figuring I already knew the answer.

"Oh, I've had better," Ralph politely said, wiping his hands on

the paper napkin and giving me a glance with his still-sparkling eyes. When Ralph was lucid and made these acerbic comments, I always laughed; I never expected his humor to be so vibrant.

"Do you want to go down the hall in your wheelchair?" I asked my elderly friend, and after considering my comment briefly, followed up with a resigned look and a nod.

Ralph pulled the wheelchair close to him, then I reached down and set the brakes. He finagled himself into the chair, reached down and released the brakes, and began to move the chair with his feet. With his head a little slumped over and weaving back and forth uncontrollably, we exited his room and headed down the hall.

"Do you want to go fast enough to mess up yer hair?" I asked.

He grunted, but didn't say anything. As we wheeled into the nurses' station, and to my surprise, Ralph yelled out, "Look who I drug in." He made me laugh.

We wheeled on down to the dining room and watched some ladies play a game of bowling on a TV set.

"Hi, Ralph!" one of the nurses yelled out, as though Ralph was the high school football star.

"Hi," came his dead-pan response, coupled with a wave of an arm.

After watching the bowling game for several minutes, he asked me to take him back to his room. We fired up his chair and moved back down the hall.

After entering his room, he removed himself from the wheel

chair and sat on the bed. He gathered the few country CDs from the table and we started to go through them.

"Who's that?" I asked.

"Waylon Jennings," Ralph answered, then began to sing, *"She's a good-hearted woman…"* Though Ralph didn't sing very well, the quality told me he once had a good voice. It was a pleasure to watch and hear him sing, and interestingly he felt comfortable enough to sing in front of me.

"I love that song. I used to listen to it a lot way back when," I shared. Ralph looked at me and kept right on singing. After watching for a few moments, I noticed his shaking became excessive; not only his hands, but his head as well.

"Are you okay?" I inquired, interrupting his singing.

He did not respond. He was shaking so hard I was thinking I should get a nurse. I could tell his body was exhausted from the shaking and unable to hold himself up.

After a moment of assessing Ralph's situation, I asked, "Do you want me to help you get into the wheelchair so you can relax?"

"I can't," he whispered. I just stood there, unsure of what to do. I offered a silent prayer, *Heavenly Father, please take away the shaking from Ralph's body.* I felt sorry for him as I watched him try to hold himself up, a difficult task with the tremors.

"Feel my arm," he instructed. I put my hand on his arm; it was hot.

"Ralph, let me help you lean against the wall so you can get the weight off of your hands." I tried to say my words with respect.

180

He nodded his head, and I guided him over near the wall so he could sit up and be comfortable at the same time. I fluffed and maneuvered a pillow behind his back. He seemed to be able to relax, and I was glad to see his eyes momentarily closed.

"You're a good man, Ralph," I softly said He didn't respond, but I could tell he got the message. "Do you want me to stay with ya?"

"As long as you want," was the reply.

With his eyes closed and his body supported, I noticed his shaking began to subside. After a few moments the tremors in both his head and hands had stopped. I knew my prayer had been answered; I was relieved he was content, even if only briefly.

His eyes remained closed, and not wanting to intrude on his rest, I whispered, "I'm going to leave now, Ralph." He cracked his eyes and nodded, and I slipped quietly out of the room.

I loved Ralph and was surprised with myself for even taking the opportunity to visit with him. Though it would appear the world no longer valued him, I took pleasure in every visit I had. He has had a profound influence on my life, and I feel blessed.

I read somewhere that grace is the unmerited gift from God that we cannot repay. So, when we give grace to others, we receive more, and hopefully, we become better people.

"Okay, boys, let's go," Mr. Reynolds announced.

Brad and I climbed into the pickup and shut the door. Mr. Reynolds, instead, stared at the ground with his hand on the

181

door handle before opening it. While watching him stand there, I realized what a great man he is. I can tell there is way more to him than meets the eye.

Mr. Reynolds opened the door and climbed in. "Well, Brad, should we see if Ma's got some supper ready?"

Brad looked up at me and I nodded my head. "Yes, sir!" he answered. "And, boy, am I hungry!"

"Well, we can't get there very fast 'til you start 'er up," Mr. Reynolds coached.

Brad looked at me and a big grin crept across his face. "Really? Do I get to start it?"

"Yes, Son, go ahead," I said, smiling. I could appreciate the excitement he felt.

Mr. Reynolds pointed to the key. "Give 'er a turn. I'm gettin' hungry." Brad turned the key and the truck started up. "Just like a well-oiled machine, don't ya think, Gary?" I nodded and thought, *yes, it sure is a well-oiled machine, alright.*

Mr. Reynolds turned out of the gas station the opposite direction from the rest area where our U-Haul was parked. A little concerned, I asked, "Shouldn't we go fix my rig, first?"

"You guys are tired, so I think a nice hot meal and a warm bed would do you a world o'good."

"That's very kind of you, Mr. Reynolds, but I'm afraid my wife will be worried when we don't show up tonight," I explained. I'm sure the concern in my voice was palpable.

"I've thought about that. I will call my friend; he's the sheriff in the area you're movin' to. He'll be off duty and won't have his uniform on, so he can go to the house and tell her what yer up to, without scarin' her. I know she won't have everything she needs to stay at the house, so we can put 'em up in a motel for the night. There's a pretty good restaurant in the motel, so she'll be able to have supper, as well. I'd rather not have you kids driving after dark, especially in a rig that's havin' issues. What's yer new address?"

I have to admit, having Mr. Reynolds offer to do so many nice things made me feel as though my own dad was watching out for us. I know my folks would be willing to help out someone in my situation.

"Well, thanks a bunch. It *has* been a long day, and I'm sure Brad is ready for something more comfy than the bench seat in that truck. I know I sure am," I stated sincerely, and ruffled Brad's hair.

I stared at the new floor mat and thought to myself, *what a kind man he is. How many people would help us like this? Those people in the Cadillac didn't even acknowledge us, much less offer to help.*

I remember once as a child, when we were driving over Lost Trail Pass at night, and came up on a pickup that was laying on its side. I remember noticing one headlight was above the other. My parents stopped and took care of the man injured in the accident; I think he had cut his head. I don't remember the details, but we took him into town where he was admitted to the hospital. I feel as comfortable with Mr. Reynolds as that man must have felt with my parents.

"How fast will this truck go, Mr. Reynolds?" Brad asked. I actually wondered that, too.

"As fast as I need 'er to," was his reply. Mr. Reynolds then down-shifted and pushed on the gas, the force pressing us against the seat. He quickly let off the gas and the truck slowed. "That fast enough for ya, Brad?" the farmer asked with a big grin.

"Wow! That was cool, huh, Dad?"

"Sure was!" I nodded methodically.

"Where do you live, Mr. Reynolds?" my son asked. Again, he and I were thinking along the same lines.

"Up here a couple of miles," he answered, pointing a crooked finger up the road.

"Do you live on a farm?" I asked. I thought he did, but I wasn't sure. Those coveralls are a telling clue. As I think back, I realized that people who've grown up on a farm are different. They seem to be more practical, especially more so than those who live in the city. They make poor bureaucrats, though. They tend to worry less about the process and more about the end result.

"Yep, I do, Gary, but I decided to quit farming when they brought the interstate highway through here. Cut through my property, made it too hard to farm."

Something in his answer triggered a guts-deep emotion in me. I sat in silence and looked out the window at the passing objects, not having a clue how to respond to his words.

"Brad, ya see that light there?" Mr. Reynolds again pointed his crooked finger down the road.

"Yes?" Brad answered, waiting to find out what came next.

"That's where I live. Just over this little rise, there is an interchange and we'll turn off there. I'm sure you passed it earlier today." He flipped on the signal and we veered onto the off-ramp. After driving a few more minutes, we turned onto a paved cul-de-sac about the length of two football fields, and approached the house. The home, or farmhouse rather, is large and stately-looking. It has a three-car garage and a large shop in the back; a very impressive property.

Mr. Reynolds parked the truck in front of the garage. Two dogs came running up to his door and when he opened it, they jumped up and began licking his arm. I noticed one was a large, rough-looking mutt and the other a black Lab. I was a little intimidated by the larger dog. "He's alright," Mr. Reynolds asserted. "You can get out. Any friend of mine is a friend of his."

We climbed out of the truck and the dogs immediately came over to check us out. The mutt jumped up and put his paws on my chest. *Wow, this dog is solid,* I thought, and was glad I distracted him as Brad climbed down. With the dogs dancing around our legs, we entered the house. A silver-haired woman greeted us with a lovely smile.

"Ma, I would like you to meet Brad and Gary Haley. I found them along the road in a bad state of repair, you might say," he explained, and kissed his wife on the cheek. "Boys, this is my lovely bride."

Mrs. Reynolds acted embarrassed by her husband, but I could tell she still had stars in her eyes for the old farmer. "Pleased to meet you! Have you had any supper?"

"Honey, that's why they're here," said Mr. Reynolds, as he peeked into the pots on the stove. "They're drivin' a movin' truck that has some fixable problems. I thought they should

185

stay the night, so they don't have to drive in the dark."

"Well, I'm glad you brought them here. I'd hate for something to happen this late at night. They can stay in the guest room," Mrs. Reynolds stated with no uncertainty. "I'll fix up the bed and linens right after dinner."

Surprisingly, it didn't even seem to be an issue, as though strays being brought home happened all the time.

As I glance around the house I notice its simple beauty. Yes, it is obviously a very expensive house, but at the same time feels like home. I guess I really didn't expect Mr. Reynolds to have such a nice home as this.

"If you boys will wash up, I'll get supper on the table. That goes for you too, Edward." She grinned at him with a gleam in her eye.

Mrs. Reynolds reminded me of all the women who influenced my life. I can tell right away she is a kind and loving person. It's easy to tell with some people, even after just a few minutes of talking with them.

We did as instructed, washing up and returning to the table.

"Brad, if you will sit over here by Ma, and Gary, if you'll sit here by me, as soon as Ma lights, she can offer the blessing."

As I listened to Mrs. Reynolds give the blessing, I thought how she reminded me of Hank's wife. After a sincere prayer, Mrs. Reynolds looked up and said, "It's nice to have you in our home." I was moved by her comment and offered a smile.

Just then the front door opened and it sounded like someone entered.

"It must be Jason," Mrs. Reynolds announced. A young man walked up to the table, and offered Mrs. Reynolds a kiss on her cheek.

As she placed her hand on the young man's face, she asked, "Hi, Jason. Have you had any supper?"

"No, Mom," answered the young man who was sporting a beard and long black hair. He had a shirt on that said "Make Love, Not War."

"Hi, Dad," he said, squeezing his father's shoulder.

"Hi, Son," the farmer said with cheer.

"Who are your dinner guests?" Jason asked.

"This is Gary and Brad Haley. And this is my son, Jason," Mr. Reynolds explained, doing a fine job with the introductions.

"Welcome to our home, Gary," said Jason, offering me his hand, so I stood up to shake it. "What brings you here, Gary?" he asked, as he pulled his chair up to the table.

"We're moving to the area and our truck broke down. Your dad was kind enough to give us a ride to the gas station, and brought us here for the night," I explained, "and we sure are grateful for the hospitality."

"Well, it's nice to meet you and Brad. I'm very lucky to have been blessed with such great parents." I could tell the way Jason spoke, he meant what he said. I nodded in agreement.

As I occasionally glanced at Jason, he seemed like he had something on his mind, but couldn't come right out and say it.

I wondered why he had the long hair and beard, why he chose the shirt he was wearing, and what his mother thinks of the boy she raised. We all sat in silence for a few minutes and focused on the delicious meal prepared for us.

Finally Jason said, "I suppose you're wondering why I'm here." Actually, I wasn't, but I allowed him to continue, uninterrupted. "I live here because I just got divorced."

I could sense some uncomfortable tension in the room. I didn't know what to say, so I just sat there in silence. I wasn't expecting to have Jason spill his life story onto the table; it was easy to see this was an open wound.

"Jason is a good man," the elder Reynolds informed us, gripping his son's shoulder. "I'm real proud of how he's gotten through some unfortunate circumstances."

"My wife...my ex-wife," he corrected, "got into drugs, and I couldn't get her off them. I don't have any children, so I guess that's good," Jason stated, swallowing hard.

Since he was so open about it, I decided to ask, "Jason, how long have you been divorced?"

"About two months," he answered.

We finished dinner, which concluded with some apple pie and ice cream we enjoyed in the living room. There was a big portrait of Jason on the wall. *He must be their only child,* I thought to myself; I saw no pictures of any other children.

It is obvious the way he and his parents treat each other, their love for him is strong. Naturally, I guess, they overlook his clothing and manner of appearance. My conscience stung me as I heard

188

what I was thinking. This time it wasn't Joyce scolding me; I did it myself.

Once our dessert was finished, Mr. Reynolds excused himself and went into his office to "finish up some paperwork."

"Brad, would you like to come with me?" Mrs. Reynolds quietly invited, and the two retreated to the kitchen. I've no doubt her mother's intuition honed in on Jason needing to talk, so she was clearing the way. It's really strange, because I have only known him for about an hour. I guess I'm closer to his age and he feels comfortable enough to ask my opinion. Something inside told me it was a way I could offer help to someone in need, as I had been helped so much today.

We sat together on a big couch which faced a massive fireplace. "What a beautiful home," I said softly, hoping to break the ice for Jason.

I look at this young man sitting with me and notice the resemblance he has to the bum I saw along the interstate earlier today. Maybe it's a similar look of hopelessness on his face, as well as the long hair. I start to feel guilty for all the things I have thought about people like him.

"Gary, it's good to have you here. I don't mean to make you uncomfortable, but I need someone to talk to. My folks have been great through all of this, but I feel like I need to give them a break. I hope you don't mind," Jason shared.

I felt like I was forming a bond with him, similar to Larry, the carnival worker I had met earlier in the day. I felt a bit uncomfortable, not just because of the nature of his situation or because I was unsure I could help him, but also the guilt from my judgmental thoughts. *I suppose if I can't add anything worthwhile, at*

189

least I can be a sounding board, I figured. As I think about it, I have had some experience being a sounding board and I suppose I can relate to most people.

I point to a picture on the wall. "When was that taken?"

"While I was in college at American University." Jason answered.

"Oh, what was your major?"

"I received my Masters in International Law, recently." It was good to see the pride in his eyes as he told me, and his tenacity was impressive. He continued, "The life with my wife was so upsetting, after graduating I took up my parents' offer to live with them until I can get on my feet."

"You know, I have no doubt it feels strange to be divorced. Sounds to me like you did all you could to salvage the marriage," I started. "It takes both partners to make it work, and if one isn't willing, the other has to walk away, I suppose. I consider my marriage to be very strong, but we've certainly had our struggles. I lost my job not too long ago, but I believe I've regained my confidence."

"How, Gary? How do you bounce back from adversity?" Jason's eyes pleaded for my help.

"Well…," I began, pausing for a moment, "I guess I just focus on what's in front of me, instead of what's behind me. It's like driving that U-Haul; if I keep looking in the rearview mirror at where I've been, I'm likely going to cause myself some serious problems with what's ahead of me. I try to remember what I ran into in my past, but I don't *expect* the road to always be filled with problems. I'm just better prepared if something does happen." Jason's eyes dropped to the floor. We sat in silence; it felt right so

I didn't try to impose on it.

I can only imagine how devastating it would be to be divorced. Jason's plight is making me look at Joyce in a more grateful way. I'm blessed to have her in my life, and I know I'm not the easiest fella to live with. To consider how people can fall out of love with their spouse is curious to me. Obviously, in Jason's case when drugs entered the equation, everything changed for him. I'm beginning to feel compassion for Jason that I admittedly did not feel when passing the bum on the interstate. Thankfully, I can only imagine how devastating losing a wife to drugs would be. I would assume that in some sort of way, he still thinks of how she was and what was in her heart when he married her.

As I look at Jason, I notice — as with Mike and Vonda — his appearance no longer captures my attention. In fact, considering the events of today, it is fascinating to realize how one's focus on the inside can blind them to what they saw on the outside.

Jason and I moved on to new conversation about what life in the United States was becoming. Mr. Reynolds entered the room and Jason looked up at him, smiling.

"Do you gentlemen mind if I join you?"

"Not at all, Dad," Jason said. "We were just talking about the government. You and I have talked about this before, Dad; I was just getting ready to tell Gary that in 1933, the United States incurred so much debt it went bankrupt, and that during President Roosevelt's years of service, he collected all the gold from the people and implemented a fine for anyone found to be in possession of gold. After the gold was collected, the government put it in Fort Knox — or at least that's what they tell us."

"Really?" I responded, never having heard the information before.

"Yessiree, Gary," Mr. Reynolds said, continuing the lesson. "The gold was then replaced with Federal Reserve notes and checkbook money, and that is what we have today. You still have that dollar?" Mr. Reynolds inquired.

Curious at the request, I reached in my shirt pocket and walked across the room, handing the paper currency to Mr. Reynolds. Taking the dollar he said, "Gary, this dollar is totally worthless."

I was intrigued. "What do you mean?"

"As you know, it is made of paper and is only worth what the paper is worth."

"Really?" I repeated.

"It's not backed by gold, but I'm sure you thought it was valuable, or at least a dollar's worth," he continued.

"Yes, I did," I replied, looking forward to what Mr. Reynolds would say next.

"Our dollar is measured in exchange rates of currencies of other countries," the farmer explained. "It is affected by interest rates, a country's debt level, and strength of its economy. It's important to remember, Gary, many things in this life are not what they seem, and that includes people, too."

As I absorbed the tutorial, my mind began to wander back through all the people who have affected my life; Hank, Ralph, and all the rest. In so doing, the admiration I've acquired for Jason, his dad, and all Mr. Reynolds has so profoundly stated caused shame

to creep into my heart. It was blatantly obvious; I, more often than not, have misjudged others.

We tend to judge people and events from what we see and hear; but it is the side we don't always observe — *the other side* — upon which we must focus. The not-always-landscaped side is where to find the greener grass, the happier people, the deeper relationships; the genius of giving, rather than taking.

CHAPTER 13
HOME

196

"To be honest, I believe I do."

"You're a good man, Gary," Mr. Reynolds yelled as we pulled away from the rest area where the moving truck had been waiting for us all night. I wondered why he was telling me that. Did he sense I needed to hear it or was it really his opinion?

As I guided the truck into the center of an interstate traffic lane, my eye was drawn to the reflection of the rising sun in the rearview mirror. It appears motionless in the morning sky as it begins its daily trajectory towards the ultimate destination somewhere behind the mountains ahead of me. It seems brighter today than it had for some time. Even the dashboard in front of me, with all its lights and gauges, appears cleaner than usual.

"Brad, doesn't it seem like a good day today?" I asked a still-sleepy little boy.

"Uh-huh," he answered, yawning. "I can't wait to get there so we can see Mom, Nick, Karen and Melissa."

"Are you excited to see our new house?"

Brad looked at me and smiled. I could see excitement building in him. I noticed on this journey, whenever he was getting

197

excited, he seemed to pay more attention to what he could see through the windshield.

"Yup! Dad, do I get my own room?" my oldest asked.

"Where would we put Nick?"

"He could sleep in the garage." Brad's face produced a smirk.

"How would you like it if Nick said that about you?"

"You know he would, Dad," Brad replied and gave me an expression that conveyed I should know this.

"Ya, he probably would."

I mulled over the question I had just posed about Brad discounting his younger brother, and being treated poorly in return. *I don't believe I have treated people the way I wanted to be treated.* My thoughts reflected back to Larry who stopped and helped us. I know I wouldn't have been as inclined or comfortable to help him as he was with me. I probably would have done something, but it most likely would've been minimal. With both hands on the steering wheel, I began to think of how Larry has enriched my life. An involuntary smile crept across my face. He is a great human being, an instant friend, and one who taught me about looking on the inside. It *should* be common knowledge to those who claim to be Christians and study the Bible, to know what is said of the Savior:

> *"The Lord seeth not as man seeth; for man looketh upon the outward appearance, but the Lord looketh on the heart." 1 Samuel 16:7*

There are probably many reasons for this, but one that I have considered recently is, when we judge others, we are often unaware

of all the facts, leaving our judgments inaccurate and damaging to those on the receiving end. The nugget in this wisdom for me is, what have I done to myself because of my inaccurate views about other people? What stereotypes have I implemented in my own mind, causing me to miss out on some likely incredible relationships? And what does my "grass" look like to the person on the other side: lush and green, or dry and brittle?

I thought to myself how wonderful today is. I reflect back on how Mr. Reynolds treated me. He is my friend, and surprisingly, I have only known him a short time. I thought, *I'm sure the fact Mr. Reynolds not only purchased the needed materials to repair the truck, but got underneath it with me helped solidify the friendship.* He came to our rescue as people are sometimes sent to do. It was a great opportunity to have met such a kind man, very intelligent, and someone I would like to emulate. *It would be great if people thought of me as I do him.*

I thought of how kind my father was when I was home. When we would go to family reunions, all the nephews, cousins and grandkids would come to Dad and he would talk with and tease them. To this day, I struggle with being interrupted by any child when I am having a conversation with an adult, especially when the person I am talking to is distracted by them. Unlike me, my parents knew everyone's name at any reunion I ever attended. For me, however, it wasn't important. Only if someone crossed my path with some purpose in my life did I pay attention to them; if not, I didn't — they were more like objects than people. I need to keep in mind what someone once stated: If you *want* a friend, you must *be* one.

Sitting in the driver's seat of this bulky vehicle, my mind reflects back on the farmers who came to the store every day. While I think about them often, today seems different. I now have a more conscious respect for them that, up 'til now, has

been suppressed for some time, a habit that began back in the days when I thought I was "cool." After all, I can't be cool if I'm seen hanging around farmers, the way they dress and speak and all. Speaking of being cool, I remember on a number of occasions when my mother would take me to school; I found myself embarrassed when she would drop me off in front of the building where *everyone* was walking. That was bad enough, but I'd get really embarrassed if she rolled down the window to speak with a student or a teacher that may be passing by. Now, I am proud to be seen with my parents, but as painful as it is to admit, back then I was not.

The farmers were always kind to me and helped when the opportunity presented itself. I remember on one occasion when I had car troubles, Zeb Jackson stopped and helped get my car running again. I have a clear picture of his partially-mashed hand attempting to remove the wingnut that secured the air cleaner to the top of the engine. Though clumsy, his smashed hand, in concert with the other, seemed to know how to get the engine running.

Yep, the farmers knew my parents, and neighbors watched over each other's children. Though it was a simple thing, I will never forget how those farmers made me feel. I remember one year when my dad was sick, some of the farmers who met at the store came to our house with their equipment, and baled and stacked the hay for him. I guess what I'm saying is, I didn't think much of it then, because that's just what farmers did for each other, like a cultural thing or something. Not until coming to the city and seeing that people didn't pay much attention to their neighbors did I realize they were intentional acts of kindness.

Though I never let on, I always knew those small town farmers didn't need to come to the Colonel's store to get coffee — they could have made their own at home or brought it in a thermos. The reason they met almost daily was to have a place away from

the house, where they could enjoy each other's company; a place to share ideas, philosophies, and common interests in a non-threatening environment.

They were realistic; they would tell it like it is, no sugar-coating, whatever "it" might be. In no way were they compelled to put on a show or try to impress anyone. Why spend all the money and energy trying to impress someone, when you have all you need? The only people who feel the need to be impressive or impressed are those who only look on the outside. Those coveralls were to work in, not to win people over. I think when we try to impress anyone, it is largely for the purpose of attempting to validate our own self-worth. Those old boys didn't need a tie to look important or drive a fancy car to get looks. A friend once told me: *Put a monkey in a silk suit, you still got a monkey.* I guess that phrase kind of stung when I first heard it. I like to wear a coat and tie to work occasionally, so maybe those words apply to me.

One character trait I felt the farmers were lacking was pride. As far as I was concerned, if they had it, they kept it under wraps. I suppose it was possible they held it inside, but there was no evidence from the outside of pride in themselves and their accomplishments; at least not how I defined "pride."

While staring out the windshield at the vanishing point of the freeway, I felt my face beginning to get hot. A number of emotions began to swell within me. Sadly, I began to realize that pride has been a significant part of my life; a guiding principle, you might say. Admittedly, I have nurtured and cultivated this long-time companion. My mind raced back to all those people I misjudged. I also was reminded of the passage in the Bible when the Savior said to one of His apostles, someone would betray Him, to which one humbly inquired, "Lord, is it I?" Since I believe the Bible is a vast fountain of wisdom from

which we can partake, I have to pose the question to myself: *Is it I, Lord? Have I not caused or contributed to the problem or misunderstanding? When I have pointed fingers to others in an accusatory or judgmental posture, do I not share in some or all of the responsibility for my uninformed declarations?* To be honest, I believe I do.

Peering through the glass that prevents the 70mph wind from entering the cab, my eyes fall on the vehicles traveling in the opposite direction. Life, in some respects, emulates the bi-directional traffic on this freeway. The traffic on the other side is heading away from us and is largely oblivious to me or the truck in which I am riding. Conversely, riding on this side of the freeway affords me to be totally indifferent to them, as well. Though not realistic, I think we tend to believe the median between us — covered with indigenous sage brush and a few wayward pop cans and beer bottles — actually protects us from vehicles on the other side.

Likewise as pedestrians, when we pass each other in a hallway, on a sidewalk, or at the market, we are unlikely to engage a stranger through eye contact or verbal interaction, thereby creating a personal median between us we may consciously or subconsciously refuse to cross. I'm starting to see I have missed out on a lot by not crossing that median.

I have always tried to be cool, hoping people would see me in the same light that I saw "professional" people. One of the obvious attributes of being cool is any form of humility has to be discarded. It is essential that a level of aloofness be indelibly etched in our persona. Someone can be perceived as cool and not be likable. I'm afraid, because of some of my behaviors throughout my life, I have been neither.

I began thinking about the leper colonies I have read about in the Bible. When you think about it, aren't leper colonies from ancient times simply a representation of how we ostracize each other

today? After all, don't some of us shun people because of their dress, income level, social status, appearance, or the neighborhoods where they reside? Do you think the emotional pain of dwelling in a leper colony is any different than the pain of being intentionally banished from the social circles we rely on for comfort and acceptance? How many of us would admit, at some point in our lives we have been involuntarily compelled to reside in proverbial leper colonies, which may or may not be temporary residency, while others are permanent?

As we move down the highway, I become conscious of the many fields under cultivation, with maturing crops and the smell of fall in the air. It is apparent I have not taken time to smell the roses or enjoy the scenery. More specifically, I have not taken the time to meet people, especially the down-trodden. Everyone has a story, everyone has value, and everyone is vulnerable whether they like to admit it or not. I wonder sometimes, if the biggest, loudest and most obnoxious people — those with whom we naturally tend to avoid — aren't the ones who struggle the most, and are actually trying to reach out to those who are quiet and seem to have confidence.

I remember an occasion when I was in the eighth grade; a friend of mine and I were sitting in the library. He made the comment that adults are just children in old bodies. How simple, yet profound. When I think about it, nothing really changes when we advance from youth to adulthood. We are still, I believe, significantly in bondage to the environment and experiences of our past. Unless we expose those undesirable hangups and biases accumulated and learn how to move beyond them, they accompany us to the grave.

"Hey, Dad, don't those green signs mean we are getting close?" Brad asked, pointing to the upcoming exit signs.

"They do," I replied, smiling without effort.

I was becoming excited for this trip to be complete. I quickly glanced around the cab of the truck, observing the dash lights, the unused cigarette lighter, the handle that opens the butterfly window, the gear shifter and steering wheel — which have been close companions along the way — and the stationary needle of the speedometer, which kept my attention throughout the journey. *I have learned a lot about life in this cab*, I mused. As boring as the inside of a truck cab is, it seems like a special place just now.

As those pretty green signs came into focus I realize, once I reach my destination, I will likely never be in this particular truck again. Pushing up on the signal lever, I begin to decelerate as the approach to the off-ramp invited me to turn. This off-ramp will mark a new beginning for me, a change of life, in more ways than one.

We exit the off-ramp and move towards town. How exciting to be a part of this community. *This will be fun*, I thought. Joyce was not anticipating this move as I have been. I feel as though I will have a great opportunity to progress.

"Dad, look at that man over there," Brad said, as he pointed to a man sitting on a bench with his head in his hands. Surprisingly, I immediately felt compassion for him.

"Dad, can we stop at this service station? I want to get a candy bar, and maybe some for Mom, Nick, Karen, and Melissa. Can we?"

"Sounds like a nice idea, Son."

I pull the truck into a befitting space, climb down, and walk into the service station. Brad picked up the appropriate number of

candy bars, and we walked up to the counter. I looked in my wallet, but couldn't find any cash. *Guess I'll have to use my credit card.* As I pay for the candy, the bells hanging from the door handle chime and alert me to someone else walking in.

"Let's go, Dad," my son said, enthusiastically. We walk between the gas pumps toward the truck.

"Brad…" I began, but was interrupted.

"Sir," came a voice behind me, and I turn to see who it is. "I think you left this on the counter."

In the doorway of the station, I spot a man holding my credit card with a big smile on his face. I immediately notice he has a tattoo on each arm, was well built, sporting a ponytail, and had a cigarette in the other hand. Without hesitation, I walk back to where the gentleman is standing. He reaches out to hand me the credit card; I reach out my left hand to take the card and the other to shake his hand.

"Hi, my name is Gary Haley," I stated.

He put the cigarette in his mouth and shook my hand with a strong grip. "Dan Foley. Good to meet you, Gary."

"Thanks for rescuing my credit card." I said. "I should have been more careful."

"I knew you would need it by the look of your rig, there. Glad to be of service to you. 'Gary, will you excuse me for a minute?"

"Sure."

Dan walked over to an ashtray made from an old milk can; while breathing out the last puff of his cigarette, he pushed and turned the remaining portion until it was out. He then walked back to where Brad was standing, bent down a little and asked, "Young man, what is your name?"

"Brad Haley," my boy answered.

I thought to myself, *what a polite gesture*. I don't follow smokers very closely, but I have never seen someone put out a cigarette just to introduce himself to a child. I appreciated his classy move.

"It looks to me like you and your dad are moving here. Am I right?"

"Yes!" Brad exclaimed, with chocolate from his candy bar melting in the corners of his mouth.

"Well, Brad, I would like to welcome you here. I think you'll like the school. In fact, I think you are going to like this whole area. It's a real friendly place and there will be *plenty* of kids for you to play with." With Dan's words, I watched Brad's eyes light up.

"That was nice of you to say, Dan. Seems you've put my son at ease. It's not always an easy transition for kids," I stated, watching Brad wander to a tire swing hanging from a nearby tree. "I also appreciate what you did with your cigarette."

"What's that, Gary?" Dan asked, unsure.

"Snuffing it out before you talked to my son."

"Oh," he replied. For a moment, we broke eye contact.

I looked over to where a man was wiping off his windshield, and

using his fingernail to scrape off a bug or something. I suspect he's probably oblivious to the character of this man standing before me. With Dan's appearance, many would never get far enough with him to care about his character, much less discover it.

Dan looked at Brad, now swinging in an old tire swing while enjoying his chocolate bar. "Can you help your Dad move all the furniture?"

Brad looked over at me and smiled, allowing me to provide the answer.

"Yep," I said with a grin, "he gets all the heavy stuff."

"Gary, I'd be happy to help you unload your truck. If you give me your address, Val Halla and I will come by and help, if you'd like," Dan offered.

"Who's Val Halla?" I inquired. I hadn't seen anyone walk in or out of the store with him.

Dan turned and pointed to a deep red Harley Davidson parked near the edge of the service station property. It made sense he wouldn't park it where any vehicles could bump into it or throw gravel.

"That's an incredible bike!" I blurted out. "Do you mind if I look at it?"

"Be my guest, Gary," Dan answered.

We walked to where the Harley stood; *what a beautiful bike!* My mind flashed back to Mike's chopper. I thought of Mike and how I misjudged him, and how I am now accepting Dan with

little or no qualification. After all, anyone who will return a stranger's credit card and offers to help unload their belongings is probably a pretty good person. I suppose Dan could be tricking me, and simply took the opportunity to deceive me with those two acts of kindness. *No,* I said to myself, *I cannot assume that. I believe he is a good person and that's where I will leave it, until or unless something changes.*

I looked at Dan and asked, "Where does 'Val Halla' come from?"

"It means 'Viking Heaven.' I am Danish and those Vikings are my ancestors," he stated, pride beaming on his face.

As I listen to Dan, I notice he takes time to express himself, and from his mannerisms he comes across with a high level of sophistication.

"That's cool, Dan. And yes, I could use your help. It'll be my wife and my three younger children waiting for us and I'd like to give her a break. Thanks for offering, if you're sure it won't be inconvenient for you," I said sincerely, and provided him my new address.

Dan climbed onto his bike. He started Val Halla, rapped the throttle a couple of times and, as he winked at Brad, put the bike in gear.

I love that sound, I thought to myself.

"Gary, I'll see you there!" Dan yelled over the engine noise. With that, he drove onto the street. I half-expected him to roar off, quickly switching gears, but he did not.

As he disappeared around the corner, I was struck by the immediate bond I felt with him. *Where have people like Dan and Mike been all my life?* I wondered. *Why haven't they presented themselves to me earli-*

er? I stood there staring at the gas pump and noticing the hose was old and weathered. Then the thought came to me: *When the student is ready, the teacher will come.* I knew why, before today, they would not have come into my life. I wasn't ready, and I haven't *been* ready until this move. I know they have been around me for many years, but I refused to let them in. *This move seems to be a transition in more ways than one.*

As we finally reached our new home on Goodall Street, my heart began to race. *This is for real,* I thought. I don't know a soul here except Dan and the people who interviewed me. We are starting over and I feel this will be a great time in our lives. I'm starting from near-scratch and can make my life however I want it to be.

Pulling the truck in front of our new home I saw Dan sitting on his bike parked on the street near the edge of the driveway. I've no doubt he didn't want to startle Joyce with his presence, and would wait for me to introduce him properly. Joyce came out of the house with the kids, and Brad and I jumped out of the truck to greet them. Once all hugs were completed, I introduced Dan to Joyce, explaining why he was there. As I expected, Joyce was gracious and grateful to him for the help.

It didn't take long to unload the truck; Joyce had boxed and organized everything so it easily went to its ultimate destination.

After unloading the truck, Joyce brought out something cold for us to drink. Dan and I sat on the front step to talk.

"Do you mind if I smoke?" Dan asked.

"No, I don't." I thought how polite he was to ask, and noticed he seemed pretty healthy-looking for someone who smokes. "Why do you smoke?" I inquired. I felt the need to explain my

question so as not to sound judgmental. "I mean, I tried it and it made me dizzy, so I've always been curious as to the attraction."

"Gary, to be honest, it is just so addictive," Dan methodically replied. "I started when I was a kid and have just never thought I'd be able to give it up."

Unless they blow their smoke in my face, I am not offended by people with this habit. Growing up, many farmers smoked, so I guess I got used to it and didn't expect anything else. I remember many of the guys older than me would wear a t-shirt and roll the cigarette pack into their sleeve. I wasn't so much concerned about Dan smoking as I was his health.

"Dan, I know it's none of my business, but if there is any way I can help you quit, when you are ready, I would be glad to help." I looked down at the sidewalk. "I knew an awful lot of farmers whose smoking affected their breathing to the point it was difficult for them to talk. I guess I don't want it to affect your health that way, too, Dan. I know it's easy for me to say you should quit, but that's why I'm offering my help, should you ever want to try."

Dan looked at me for a second, turned his head and blew out a couple smoke rings. "Gary, I honestly appreciate your sincerity. Maybe sometime that opportunity will present itself. Can't say I've ever had anyone offer to help; thanks for speaking up."

"Well, I'm grateful for your friendship. I know our lifestyles are different, but we still have a lot in common." A somewhat-foreign emotion was beginning to express itself, and tears started to well-up in my eyes.

Seeing my emotional dilemma Dan gently stated, "I'm going to have to leave; I got a biker friend who's having some extreme anxiety problems, and I promised I'd check up on him. But, if it's okay with you and the Mrs., I'd like to come back and talk more. I'm sure you'd like to get settled into the new place, though, so don't feel obliged to let me come back." I was sure he saw the look on my face, welcoming him back to our new home.

Dan and I stood up simultaneously and we hugged. As I reached around his back, my hand fell on his ponytail...

ACKNOWLEDGEMENTS

I would like to acknowledge all those from different groups, interests and cultural backgrounds who had a profound influence on my life and from whom I learned to see the other side, instead of forming my opinion and assumptions based on casual observation.

213

214

ABOUT THE AUTHOR

 Though Paul Raymond is a native of Idaho, he spent the formative years of his life on a farm in western Montana. He later attended Ricks College and Idaho State University. Prior to retiring, his career included being a city engineer and a public works director. The motivation to write this book stems from his longtime interest in observing and working with people, always being intrigued by their differences, motives, and behaviors.

Paul has an ongoing quest to find truth. In addition to his career field, he has an interest in philosophy, religion, geology, as well as national and world history. Paul has recently been elected to the Nampa City Council, which, to his satisfaction, puts him squarely in the center of people sharing their feelings, emotions, and passions.

Paul and Connie, his wife of 44 years have four children and 11 grandchildren.

TRADEMARKS & COPYRIGHT

Caterpillar Equipment ®
Farmall ®
Harley Davidson Motorcycles ®
John Deere Tractors ®
"Take This Job and Shove It"© by David Allan Coe
"Where the Corn Don't Grow"© by Roger Murrah and Mark
Alan Springer